close

to

you

close to you

Virginia Young

Virginia Young

Riverhaven Books
www.RiverhavenBooks.com

close to you is a work of fiction. While some of the settings are actual, any similarity regarding names, characters, or incidents is entirely coincidental.

Copyright© 2019 by Virginia Young

All rights reserved.

Published in the United States by Riverhaven Books, www.RiverhavenBooks.com

ISBN : 978-1-937588-95-3

Printed in the United States of America
by Country Press, Lakeville, Massachusetts

Designed and Edited by Stephanie Lynn Blackman
Whitman, MA

"The sea belongs to us all, and every aspect of it...is fraught with beauty.

- Samuel Eliot Morison

*This novel is dedicated
to my brother Francis J. McNulty, who was lost to us
when his plane crashed on Martha's Vineyard*

Also by Virginia Young

Out of the Blue
A romance set in Massachusetts

The Birthday Gift
A romance set in Connecticut

Sleepless Tides
A romance set in Maine

Winter Waltz
A romance set in Vermont

By a Thread
A contemporary novel

Find Me
A collection of short stories and poetry

A Family of Strangers
A romantic suspense set in Canada and New Hampshire

I Call Your Name
A romantic suspense set on Martha's Vineyard

Nocturnal
A young adult novel

Where Seagulls Sleep
A romantic suspense set in Rhode Island

Annasheeva
A romance

Stone
A contemporary romance

A Midnight Bell
A contemporary suspense

Chapter One

I believe he's there. I long to tell him that I know he's there, that I think he's hiding, but then, wouldn't he also be hiding from me? I can't help but be an invasion into his life, and what right do I have there?

*****

I'd been at my *Commonwealth Journal* desk working on a list for an assigned story when my editor, Bill Sieller, came to my side. I looked up and smiled. "I'm hurrying – really I am."

"I believe you completely," he said. "But I want you to put that away for now and write something else for me. It's going to mean a little digging on your part. It's the Finnegan case you covered a year ago. The public is still interested in this man. I want a follow-up."

I leaned back in my swivel chair and swallowed hard. "Really? A whole year later?"

"Yup. People inquire about this. Some news items get under your skin. Readers look for a conclusion. He has a lot of patients who miss him, not to mention family and friends. There was no answer to his disappearance. Maybe there's still no answer, but we'll give it another try."

I nodded in agreement as Bill walked away but

wished we could leave this one alone. I'd never met Granger Finnegan but had seen multiple pictures of him – next to his plane, next to his sailboat, boyishly smiling, his light brown hair being lifted slightly in the wind, his penetrating eyes challenging the camera to capture his essence. And while he didn't fit the mold for being classified as handsome, I'd found myself captivated by him for months after covering the story. I'd begun to feel I could let go, until now.

Bill was the kind of person and editor who cared about his readers, always wanting to give the full benefit of light to a shadowed subject. When he requested work on an assignment, it was done. I wondered about this one, but I wasn't the boss.

I went to my files on Dr. Granger Finnegan and found a close up of his face. I looked at it for several minutes, causing a churning within, then retrieved the notes and the article pertaining to the plane crash. There had been this impenetrable doubt about his survival. Had he jumped from the plane before its meeting with the sea? Nothing of him was ever found – not a jacket, not a shoe, nothing. He was known for being a strong swimmer; he might have survived. I wanted to think so.

*****

Two days later, on a crisp autumn morning, I found myself driving into the heart of Wellesley, Massachusetts. I passed by the prestigious college named for that town, then watched for the house where I'd been once before, both times looking for information on the whereabouts of Granger Finnegan. I'd approached the white, over-sized Colonial structure surrounded by a white picket fence and moon gate; it was charming, true New England.

I parked my car in front of the house, dared to allow myself through the gate, and then on to the front door. Over the door, drying and faded pink roses half-heartedly lingered in the chilled air, and an invitation was written in aqua blue, one I hadn't forgotten from a full year ago, *Come to the Sea with Me*. I recalled feeling a chill the first time, and I was feeling it again. There I stood, once more beneath those six unforgettable words. I rang the doorbell and was greeted by a young woman, an attractive blonde with blue eyes, a little girl at her side.

"Mrs. Finnegan," I began, "I telephoned you earlier. I'm Cara Wells from *The Commonwealth Journal*."

"Yes," she said. "I remember you from a year ago. I'm grateful for the phone call prior to your coming. I don't really know what I can tell you. The story's been told over and over with no results. It's been very upsetting."

"I'm sure it has."

"Come in," she invited. "This is my daughter, Jill."

I smiled at the little girl who looked to be about five years of age. Inside, a Golden Retriever lay behind a

close to you

gate in the kitchen area. He looked up when I entered the living room, then put his head down on his paws as though hoping to see someone else.

"That's Prancer," the woman said. "Finn's dog. He's never been the same, devoted to Finn, tolerant of the rest of us." She gestured for me to take a seat on the sofa opposite the one where she sat down with Jill.

I felt sorry for the poor dog, he looked depressed. "Mrs. Finnegan," I began.

"Please," she said, "call me Eve."

I nodded then continued. "Eve, is there anything at all you can tell me about your husband? I know there were no conclusions when he disappeared a year ago, but has there been any new information? Has anyone come forward with a clue as to where he was going?"

Eve Finnegan looked me directly in the eyes then wrapped her arm around the timid little girl. "I don't know anything more today than I did a year ago. It's all very mysterious. It wasn't like him to take a day off from the hospital to go flying, especially to a place like Martha's Vineyard."

I was uneasy asking questions in front of the child and was careful about how I spoke.

"Was that a place you'd gone together?"

"No, not at all. Finn knew I hated it out there. I'm not an ocean person; I favor the desert."

"I couldn't help but notice the words over your front door."

"That was Finn's sentiment. He owned this house before we became a couple two years ago. I've thought about removing the saying – I just haven't gotten around to it."

So, I wondered, was this not Granger Finnegan's child? No one had alluded to her existence one year ago.

"Jill?" I began with the question in my eyes and tone.

"Jill is my daughter from a former relationship." That was all she offered.

I nodded. "How about his family? As I recall, he had very few living relatives. Have you had any contact with them?"

Eve shook her head. "There's no one really. His father is elderly, lives in a nursing home on the Cape. He doesn't recognize anyone but Finn now, so we don't visit. Finn's mother passed away several years ago, I never knew her. He was an only child, so aside from a few cousins and an aunt in Connecticut who he wasn't close to, there's no one."

"May I ask how you're coping? How has your life changed?"

Eve tugged lightly at the hem of her knee length skirt. "Nothing has changed. I try to keep things as normal as possible for Jill. She misses him, of course."

I thought how odd it was that she would not include herself in that statement. Didn't she miss her husband?

Staring at my notebook with a few scratches of information, nothing that would constitute an in-depth article for the paper, I didn't know what else I might ask. This was a well-respected Boston doctor, a neurosurgeon, who left one day, climbed into his Globe Swift plane, and disappeared in a crash.

When I returned to *The Journal* that afternoon, I sought out Bill to tell him it had been a wasted effort. He said they'd give it a front-page blurb, a simple and truthful attempt to solve the question of what happened to Dr. Granger Finnegan. I felt relieved in being able to let go of this saga. And yet the story had become part of me from the moment of its conception. I'd been known to be a persistent and thorough reporter, but something here was different. I was out of my element.

*****

A month later, in early November, I found myself driving down the same street, Route 135 in Wellesley. I was on my way to Ashland to do a report on a one-hundred-year-old man who had a garden filled with an assortment of unusually huge gourds and pumpkins. As I approached the Finnegan house, I was startled to see a *For Rent* sign posted by the picket fence. Eve Finnegan hadn't mentioned just one month earlier that she was thinking of leaving. I slowed the car then stopped. I took a few minutes, wondering if I should approach the faded invitation to the sea. I knocked on the dark blue door, but when no one responded, I turned and walked back toward my car. As I did, Prancer came bounding out to greet me from a neighbor's yard. A woman I guessed to be in her late seventies walked toward me and asked if she could help.

"Molly Penniman," she said as she offered a firm hand to shake. "You looking for Eve Finnegan?"

"Hi. I'm Cara Wells from *The Journal*. I spoke with Eve about a month ago; she didn't indicate that she might be moving. I was curious about it when passing by and saw the sign."

"Everyone's curious about it," Molly said with a husky voice. "She's gone, didn't want this poor dog, asked me to keep it until I could find it a home. Want a dog? He's a nice boy, just a lot for me to handle these days."

I knelt down to pat the gentle creature who seemed enthused with the gesture of affection.

"Do you know where she went?" I asked as I stood.

"Who knows? Off with that man of hers I guess. Don't like him much, but he's the child's father, so what can I say?"

"She went off with Jill's father? Had he been in the picture all along, before Dr. Finnegan disappeared?"

"Not regularly, but sometimes. Finn was a wonderful man. What a great neighbor. Eve came here and that ended that; I hardly got a chance to speak to Finn from that time on. I miss him, and so does this poor dog."

I looked at Molly Penniman and then at Prancer who had settled at her feet. He looked at me with a longing in his eyes; I'd been thinking of getting a pet, someone to go home to at night. My rented house was small, but I had a nice yard.

"Yeah, why not?" I said, as much to myself as to Molly. "Prancer can have a home with me."

She fetched his leash and Prancer climbed into my car as if he'd done it a thousand times before.

I thanked Molly for everything, then drove on to Ashland for the great pumpkin story. Prancer was invited into the front passenger seat and looked like a true navigator, taking in landmarks he might have known from travels with his old friend.

I thought about the Finnegan family, how strange it all was. I could have persisted in asking more when I'd had the interview with Eve, yet she seemed slightly annoyed with the few questions I'd asked. I tried to reason that it might be anxiety over Finn's loss, but she had no obvious signs of remorse. I considered talking it over with Bill, but then he'd probably ask me to further investigate to see where Eve had gone and why. Part of me wanted to drop the whole subject and part of me longed to know, with what seemed to be such an idyllic life, where everyone had gone.

By two o'clock, I was on the road back into Boston. I decided to be completely honest with Bill. I'd never been anything but, and he deserved to know what I'd learned. Besides, an animal lover, I knew he'd enjoy meeting Prancer Finnegan.

As I'd suspected, Bill was both curious and energized by the new development but thought the story was probably dead in the water. He said we'd see what developed. I agreed.

Unlocking the door to my four-room converted cottage by the sea in Prides Crossing, Prancer walked in as if he owned the place. He checked out each small room and then I took him into the yard on his leash. I could see his velvet nose rise to sniff at the salty air and then he looked at me. I decided we'd both have some baked chicken for dinner, and later, like two old friends, we shared the sofa and some mindless TV.

On Thursday evening that first week with Prancer, I had business in the Wellesley area and thought maybe I could speak to Molly Penniman again. And with Prancer by my side, I felt certain they'd enjoy seeing one another while old haunts were briefly explored. I glanced toward the Finnegan home and noticed one small light at the front door – the windows in shadow, as though no one cared about the lovely old structure.

A few moments later, I tapped on Molly's paneled door. The outdoor copper lantern bathed us in bright energy-saver light, and she appeared.

"Oh, hello again."

"I'm sorry not to have called first," I said. "I didn't

have your number with me, so I thought I'd take the chance to stop by. Prancer also wanted to say hello."

Molly gave me a brief look then stepped aside to allow her four-legged friend into the warm home. "I was just about to have some peanut butter toast and tea for my supper. Want some?"

I smiled. "That sounds wonderful."

Prancer was given toast with peanut butter also, and we laughed as he licked his mouth trying to get the sticky stuff off his tongue and teeth.

Everything in her home was decorated with roses and peonies. Molly had a way of putting orange and pink, burgundy and bright red together and making it work. I loved the warmth, the evidence of a life filled with color, zest for anything that breathed or grew. Even the cups from which we drank our Earl Grey were pale blue with pink and white peonies. The atmosphere was as delicious as the tea and toast.

"So," Molly began as she touched a napkin to the corners of her mouth, "I can see you two have bonded. Obviously you aren't here to return Prancer."

I laughed and shook my head.

"Was there some other reason for your stopping by?"

I folded my napkin next to my plate and took a sip of my tea. "I'm not even sure, Molly. This Finnegan case is perplexing. I guess I should start by asking how long you knew Dr. Finnegan."

Molly shrugged. "Pretty much all his life. Not steadily, of course. He had all those pre-med years at school and then his internship, but he always came back here when he could. That was his grandfather's house originally. This is where Finn grew up. We had this running joke..." she said with a fond remembrance in her eyes, "our names were so similar in sound, Finnegan, Penniman, he used to say someday we'd form a partnership of sorts. He suggested a farm stand where I could sell violets and he could sell radishes."

I laughed and took another swallow of warm tea. "I didn't know that house was a family home. It makes leaving the place even more significant, doesn't it?"

"Only to Finn, and he's gone. It makes me sick to think of it. He was such a dear child and a fine man. They were all good people, the Finnegans; I liked every one of them."

I wished I could see out to Molly's yard from the window where we sat, but with the darkness, I could only see our reflections in the glass – two women, eager to find a missing person, each with their own hope for his welfare. I felt I was getting too close to this story again; my journalism skills were being clouded by an emotional harness.

"Do you have any idea where he may have been heading that day? Eve told me they never went to the Vineyard; I'm curious about why he crashed so close to the island."

close to you

Molly shook her head. "Finn's mother was born to the place; his parents settled out there when they married. After Finn's mother died – he was barely nine – his father left the island and came here to the grandfather's house. George, Finn's father, disliked Eve. She, in turn, rejected anything to do with the island. It was all such a mess. Poor Finn was caught in the middle. I think he went out there sometimes to escape."

"Have you any idea why Finn's father didn't care for Eve?"

Molly half snickered. "He was getting a bit senile, but he was still wise. He could just tell what kind of woman she was, a real opportunist. She had nothing. She was raising that little girl, and at first the fellow who fathered her was nowhere in sight. Finn had operated on Jillian, then Eve latched on to Finn fast and tight. He'd never been a ladies' man type, if you get my drift. He was brilliant, but innocent. Eve seemed like anything but."

I shifted in my chair and moved my spoon from the table to the cup's saucer. "Do you think there was trouble between them?"

Molly nodded. "Can't say for sure, but it seemed like there wasn't much going on that was particularly loving. Finn was dedicated to his work, enjoyed his home, and loved that dog. Eve, well she tended to her daughter, but she was never friendly. There were days when I'd be out poking around in my yard and I'd see bags and bags of who knows what coming from the trunk of her car. I guess she liked to shop."

"It's odd, Eve renting the house and going off with Jill's father. Did she come to say goodbye?"

"In a weird manner, yes; that's how I ended up with Prancer. She told me that this Tony, Jill's father, had come back into her life when he heard of Finn's disappearance. Funny thing is, like I told you before, that guy was around for at least a few months before anything happened to Finn. She must think I'm not only old but blind."

I looked out to the darkened yard again, wishing for access to the Finnegan house just twenty or thirty yards away.

"Do you think Finn suspected something was going on between Eve and Tony?"

"Maybe," Molly agreed with a nod. "That thought crossed my mind a time or two. Finn stopped here one day during last summer's end. Brought me some of the most beautiful tomatoes and peppers I've ever seen. He'd gotten them at the market in the North End. He mentioned his plane and its antiquity, how he planned to go flying that weekend. Then he said that Eve knew someone, an old friend, who wanted to go up with him. The guy supposedly knew more about the Globe Swift than Finn did. I'm betting that old friend was Tony."

I hated feeling the way I did, but I was starting to

wonder what part, if any, Eve had in Finn's disappearance. When Finn's plane was recovered from the water, the authorities indicated that fuel lines had been severed. No one seemed to have any answers to how or why that would have happened. I'd covered every link at the time; all met a dead end.

"The house on the Vineyard, the one Finn's father left when they came here, was that sold?"

"Oh, I'm sure it was. George was so grief-stricken when Cynthia died, he never wanted to go out there again."

I reached down and stroked Prancer's neck and ears.

Chapter Two

Two weeks passed, and even though I was busy, I couldn't get the Finnegan story off my mind. That weekend I drove to Woods Hole with Prancer and took the ferry over to the island. There I rented a car from a man named Jim Donohue, an islander from birth.

"Can you recommend a place I could stay with my pal here?" I asked pointing to Prancer.

"Sure can," Jim replied. "My lovely bride of fifty-five years and I have a small motel we run out on Corbin's Beach. Not much of a beach, too rocky, but the place is clean and this time of year, we've got plenty of vacancies. Free coffee and muffins in the morning."

I smiled. "Sounds perfect."

With directions to the motel, I drove there and settled in. I'd passed a small store just before the motel with a sign in the window advertising steamed hotdogs for ninety-nine cents. I'd expected to enjoy seafood out there, but I was hungry and decided the hotdogs sounded good, for both Prancer and me. Once settled, I clipped his leash in place then we walked the half-mile

close to you

to fetch our dinner.

The next morning I woke up to seagull songs as they swirled and dipped over and into the sea in a magical formation. They were beautiful. I gave Prancer an extra hotdog and roll from supper the night before, then took him out for a stroll on the dunes above the rocks and sand. He raised his regal nose and sniffed the air as he watched the flight of at least twenty gulls. I prodded him along, urging him nearer to the office where the muffins and coffee Jim had promised were waiting.

"Well, good morning," Jim greeted me as I walked through the door. "Did you and your furry friend sleep well?"

"Wonderfully well. Is it alright for Prancer to be in here?"

"Sure is," Jim said as he poured me a coffee. "My bride will be sorry to have missed you. She just left with our eldest daughter for the mainland. They need a day of shopping now and then. They'll be back this evening. Our daughter's married to a police officer here. Our other daughter and her family live in Falmouth."

"Sounds great."

"They're the best." Jim passed me a tray of muffins. "We have blueberry and cranberry this morning. Take your pick."

I selected cranberry then sat down at a little table

with my coffee. Jim sat down across from me and patted Prancer. "This is a nice dog. I knew another dog named Prancer once a long, long time ago."

"Really? Out here on the island?"

"Sure thing. Little boy had the dog. Nice family; they've been gone for years now."

The hairs on my arms felt like metal probes. "Did they live nearby?"

"Sure did. Right around the bend from here, over at The Narrows, that strip of land right over there." Jim pointed to an area off to the right. "Fella that lives there now, he fixes broken seagulls and other hurt things. Don't know how he knows to do it, repairing those pesky birds."

I looked in the direction he'd called The Narrows, then back to Jim and Prancer. "He must like them," I said, trying to be casual.

"Sure must. Don't get me wrong: I like the gulls too. It wouldn't be home without them."

I smiled at Jim then offered Prancer a tiny piece of my muffin. "I need to buy some dog food for this handsome fellow. He's been dining on chicken and hotdogs lately."

"I'll bet he's not complaining," Jim said.

"No, I'm sure he's been enjoying it all, and he'll get more of the same, but I thought I'd pick up a good quality kibble too. Is there a store nearby, other than the little convenience store down the street?"

"Oh, sure. There's Martin's. Just take your right going out of the parking lot. Go just about three miles and swing into Martin's on your left. That's the grocery store my bride prefers. And while you're at it, diagonally across the street from Martin's, there's a place you might try for dinner – The Watermark Café. Best seafood anywhere. All the locals eat there, even the seagull guy."

I nearly choked on my last bite of muffin. I'd been trying to think how I'd meet him. "Really? Sounds like you're right about the good food."

"Oh, yes. My bride and I go there once or twice a week. I love the clams, she likes the scallops; it's a good place, and reasonable."

"Thanks, I'll keep that in mind." I wanted to inquire more about the seagull guy but decided it might be more than a stranger should find of interest.

"How long you staying out here?" Jim asked.

I looked out toward the sea and wished I could answer forever. "Just the weekend. I have work on Monday. I'm thinking I might come out again next weekend though. Could I have the same accommodations?"

Jim stood to reach for the coffee pot. "More?" he offered.

"Thanks, no; I think I'm all set."

He poured coffee into a cup for himself then sat down again. "This time of year, no problem. We can fill up around Thanksgiving, but that's a couple of weeks away. It always surprises me how many folks come out here for the holidays. I guess the atmosphere is right."

"I guess so," I agreed, then I asked, "The man who repairs the seagulls, is he a veterinarian?"

"You know, I don't think so. Just a nice fella with a fair amount of money. He bought that house on The Narrows cash. Nice man. Everyone likes him. Keeps to himself…someone said they think he's a writer."

"Oh. What's his name? Would I know his writing?"

"Can't say you'd know his work, never saw any of it, but his name is Geoff Flynn; came out here about ten, maybe eleven months ago. Said he spent time on the island as a boy, knows his way around. Nice fella."

I shivered and hoped it didn't show.

"So, you think you'll be back next weekend?"

"Yes, I'll try to come on Friday, early evening. I wish I could stay longer; maybe I will one day."

"What's your line of work?"

"I work for *The Commonwealth Journal*," I said and that seemed to be enough information. From morning coffee with Jim, Prancer and I drove to Martin's for dog food, two bowls for food and water, and some gourmet dog treats. I took a long look at The Watermark Café, its pale gray exterior with white trim and flower boxes overflowing with English Ivy. That evening, I'd leave Prancer with an ample dinner at the motel and check out The Watermark's fare. And, if I was lucky, Geoff

Flynn.

I hadn't brought anything exciting with me for clothing, but I had a pretty blue jersey I wore with jeans. My freshly washed hair had a decent swing to it against my shoulders – I was okay. I walked into the café and was invited to sit wherever I liked. I chose a small table over-looking the dunes and the sea, illuminated by a floodlight off the back of the small building.

The waitress brought me water and I ordered a glass of white wine before browsing the menu. I took a clue from Jim and ordered his wife's favorite, scallops, broiled with a side of coleslaw.

Everyone who came through the door was in my sight. I looked at my watch. I couldn't stay there forever, but I could eat slowly. I checked the time, six forty-five. My meal arrived and so did Geoff Flynn. When he walked in, he looked thinner than his photos from a year ago, and now he wore glasses, but I was confident that I'd just seen a ghost.

"Geoff," the bartender greeted him, "your usual?"

I ate my dinner as calmly as possible, my eyes diverting to him often. What made him run?

Prancer and I spent that Sunday walking the island's coastline, taking in the rushed sound of the waves embracing the shore with a determined energy. I hated to leave Monday morning on the early ferry, but I had no choice.

Prancer and I made our way from Woods Hole to Prides Crossing in about three hours. I made it to work late, but at least I was there. Later that afternoon, I felt restless with the need for more information. I went back to the files on Dr. Granger Finnegan and recalled that he had a good friend, someone who also owned a Globe Swift plane. The man, Derek Halstrom, lived in Plymouth. I'd tried to contact him a year ago but he was out of town on business. Determined to try again, that Monday evening I called him.

"I'm surprised to get a call about Finn after all this time," he said into the phone, children's voices in the background.

"Yes, it's been a while. It's just that my editor has had inquiries from several readers, so we thought we'd follow up if we could."

"Well," Derek said, "he was a heck of a guy. I miss him. Other than that, I'm not sure what I can offer."

"How long had it been since you'd seen him before his crash?"

"Less than a week. We'd flown together on the weekend. I was surprised when he went out again so soon. He normally only got down this way about once a month between work and family obligations."

"Down this way? Did he fly in the Plymouth area often?"

"Yeah. Most times we flew to the Cape, out to the Vineyard, or sometimes to one of the other New

England states. We had our favorite jaunts."

"Is there anything unusual you can remember about that week when you saw him last?"

There was a hesitation from the other end of the line. "He seemed distracted, said something about a guy who had an interest in his plane. Finn wasn't interested in selling...he loved that thing. It was all kind of strange. It almost sounded like Finn felt threatened. I never really knew. That wife of his was a piece of work, I can tell you that. Poor guy was miserable from about one month after saying 'I do.'"

"Were you at their wedding?

"No, didn't even know about it until after it happened."

Having spoken with Eve Finnegan, I wasn't surprised. I only knew Granger Finnegan through others' eyes, but I'd met Eve on two occasions and found her cold.

"Do you have any idea why he was miserable?"

I heard Derek sigh. "I'm not sure. Apparently the little girl's father was a tough guy; Finn had the idea he was mob material. Who knows?"

"Did you know that Eve left the house, that it's up for rent?"

"*What?*"

I closed my eyes for a moment then opened them and confirmed he'd heard right. "She's gone. She left the dog with a neighbor to find him a home."

"Unbelievable," Derek said. "Finn loved that dog. I'd bet anything that she and that guy went off on Finn's dollar. Money was never an issue there, but I'll bet it ticks her off that she can't sell the house too. With a missing person case, there's a waiting period I guess."

"Yes, I'm sure you're right."

"So, any idea where the dog is?"

"He's with me," I replied.

"Good. That's great. I'm glad he has a good home."

When I hung up with Derek Halstrom, I sat for at least thirty minutes, Prancer at my side. I couldn't stop thinking about Geoff Flynn living out on The Narrows, taking care of wounded birds. I hoped my workweek would be a busy distraction; I couldn't wait to get out to the Vineyard the coming weekend.

*****

When I arrived there on Friday evening, this time armed with plenty of dog food, I rented a car again from Jim and drove out to the motel. My room was ready, warmed and with a complimentary muffin waiting for me. I'd had a slice of pizza on my way from Boston to the ferry, but the muffin looked good. On a two-plate electric stovetop, I made myself a cup of coffee, gave Prancer a few snacks, changed into warm pajamas and slippers, switched on the TV, then sat on the bed where Prancer joined me.

Saturday morning I woke up to the cry of gulls. I

stretched and felt glad to be in my small room on this wonderful island. With an urging from Prancer, I slipped shoes on my feet and a coat over my pajamas to take him out for a brief walk. After that, I fed him and then took a warm bath. I needed time to figure out what I was doing next.

After drying myself off and changing into jeans and a warm sweater, Prancer and I went into town. I found a place to park where I could see him from the restaurant window and went in to place an order for eggs and toast for two. Prancer liked people food; eggs once in a while wouldn't hurt him. We drove toward the beach, parked, and ate. After that, I took Prancer for a ten-minute walk. It was cold and blustery; we were both happy to get back into the car.

We drove around for a while, then turned toward the motel and the area Jim referred to as The Narrows. I drove slowly by the home of Geoff Flynn but saw no sign of life. We went back to the motel around noon where I sat and thought. What did I hope to accomplish? How would I tell Bill? *Would* I tell Bill? Maybe I had no business in this man's life.

Something kept nagging at me. Was Geoff really Finn as I believed he was? I wanted him to be because I wanted him to be alive. If it was him, he'd elected to leave his life, his career, and even his beloved dog. What drove him away?

That night, I went to The Watermark Café in the

hopes that I'd see him again. The place was crowded; I decided not to stay. I drove to a smaller place that advertised take-out and pulled into the parking lot. As I did, a dark blue station wagon pulled up next to me and when the driver's eyes met mine, it was a brief but immediate recognition. My heart felt like it had fallen to my feet, but I forced myself to pick up an order of scallops and drove back to the motel where I shared a few with Prancer. I was angry with myself for becoming so anxious about coming face to face with Geoff Flynn. That's what I'd been hoping for, and now I was running away. Sunday morning, I left. I wanted to stay but felt the true need to go. I needed more time and space from this perplexing situation.

Driving back to Prides Crossing, I felt more and more ill at ease. Part of me was back on that island. Maybe that's what frightened me. What was I doing?

Sunday night, I did some research for a different story I needed to write for *The Journal*, then took a hot shower and went to bed. I lay there for some time, trying not to wish that I was on Martha's Vineyard. I hated the feeling of being divided, yet I was. Again, I hoped for a busy week to keep my mind occupied, and I wasn't so sure about the coming weekend. The Thursday after was Thanksgiving, just a week and a half away, and I wasn't sure what I was doing about that either. Mom and Dad were expecting me to show up with my green bean casserole and a chocolate cake. I guessed I'd go, but there was still that weekend before.

When I got home from work Tuesday evening around six, I took Prancer out for his duty call then opened a can of food for him. I popped a frozen potpie in the microwave and checked my phone messages. Mom had called to make sure I was still arriving Thursday pre-noon; a friend in Texas was checking in; and there was a not-too-clear message from Molly Penniman. I listened to it again then called her.

"Hi Molly, it's Cara. I just got your message. Where did you say the inquiry came from?"

"I can't be one-hundred percent," she began, "but I'd swear it was Finn's voice. The man said he'd driven by the house, that he'd seen the sign, and he wondered if I knew what had happened to the dog."

I closed my eyes and swallowed hard. "Wow," I said softly. "That's interesting. Did you tell him that I have Prancer? And have you mentioned this to anyone else?"

"Nope, not a soul. I didn't get a chance to talk to him, it was a message. I'd probably have told him you had taken Prancer and that he was just fine. If he calls back, do you want me to tell him? I mean, I'm not positive who the caller was – I want it to be Finn, but you know it might not have been. I know you love that dog; I don't want you to think you have to give him up."

I looked at Prancer who had curled up next to me on

the sofa ready for a little TV.

"I'm glad you told only me. We're thinking the same on this subject. If he calls again, give him my number. I'm curious. And, like you, I want this man to be Finn. How are you anyway? What are you doing for Thanksgiving? Big plans?"

"Oh, I'm fine. No plans for turkey day. I recall some great holidays, but since my husband's passing and my son's move to New Mexico, I pull out the memories and I don't feel so alone. Some people don't have good memories; I do, and I feel lucky to have them."

I was thinking while listening and it didn't take much time for me to issue an invitation. "Come to my family's with me Thanksgiving morning. With you, there will be ten of us. Mom and Dad would love it if I brought someone, and she's a great cook."

"How far away?"

"About an hour from Wellesley. I could pick you up around ten, get to Mom and Dad's around eleven, have some of Dad's killer eggnog, and dinner at two. We'd be back in Wellesley by seven, eight at the latest. You'd love it."

There was a distinct hesitation from Molly then, "Why not? But only if I can bring a contribution or two. I like to cook. You might not think so since I often have toast and peanut butter for supper, but I get lazy, and I like peanut butter. I make a whopper of a cheesecake, and my cranberry salad is extremely good."

I laughed. "Great. I won't try to discourage your offerings – that cheesecake will be perfect. Now back to that call for a moment. Did he leave a number, anything?"

"No. The answering machine is an old thing and it cut part of what he said, but I could swear to goodness it was Finn's voice."

"Okay, let's just see what happens. I'll pick you up about ten on Thanksgiving. Be hungry, and prepare for a feast!"

*****

The rest of my week was mud. All I wanted to do was hear again from Molly regarding Finn, or rush into the weekend and another couple of days at the Vineyard.

I left work at one on Friday, picked Prancer up at home, and drove to Woods Hole for our ocean journey to the island. The routine was set. I picked up the car from Jim, stopped for one of Prancer's hotdogs, then on to the motel. It was beginning to feel like home.

It was cold on the island. November winds and forty degrees were a tough mix. At the motel, Prancer and I found our room warm and welcoming, a muffin waiting on the small table. Glad to settle in for the evening, Prancer and I watched TV from the bed and I called my mother to talk about Molly and my standard contribution to our Thanksgiving feast.

Saturday morning sunshine came as a surprise. I'd fallen asleep with the TV on, Prancer by my side. As soon as he saw my eyes opened, he jumped off the bed and sat by the door: a subtle hint. I slipped my coat on as I stepped into my shoes then headed for the door with the leash. A few minutes outside, the cold wind lifting my collar, was enough to make Prancer content. He willingly came back into the room where I dressed and combed my tousled hair. Prancer had a can of his food and some water then we headed to the office for real coffee, not the instant I had in my room. I walked in and found an attractive older woman placing muffins onto a glass plate, its glass dome off to the side.

"Good morning. You must be Cara. I'm Mary Donohue."

"It's nice to meet you. You have a wonderful place here, and I'm so grateful that you allow pets. I couldn't stay if Prancer wasn't welcome."

"Of course. I understand completely. We have two cats, and they're family."

I smiled as Mary offered me coffee and a muffin. "Are these chocolate chip?" I asked, pointing to a third choice.

"Yes, they are. Every once in a while I enjoy having something different to offer our guests, even though the blueberry and cranberry are favorites."

I helped myself to the chocolate chip muffin and a

hot coffee, then sat down to enjoy my breakfast, Prancer looked longingly for a nibble, which he got.

"You've been out here several weekends. Are you thinking of moving here?"

That thought hadn't occurred to me at all. "No, I work in Boston and that's a must for now. It's just so pure and wonderful here. I love spending time on the island."

"You should come when it's warm," she said with a smile. "It's lovely here in the mild months."

"I've actually been here when it's warm. My family used to come out over the week of July fourth. That was when you could still rent a place and not have to forfeit your life's savings."

Mary nodded and smiled. "I know. Rents have gone sky high; it's ridiculous."

"I was wondering about that strip of land called The Narrows. Is that private property?"

"Yes and no. That property was once owned by one family. When they left the island many years ago, the piece upon which the house sits was kept private. The remaining parcel of land, dunes, and beach was given to the island and is public."

"I see. So I can walk there? It looks like an inviting hike for Prancer and me."

"It's craggy and beautiful over that way, but watch your step – lots of rocks and none too even."

We chatted for another few minutes then Mary

needed to take a phone call. I waved goodbye and left with Prancer who was always eager to go.

I stood outside the office on a flagstone patio, looking northeast toward The Narrows. I wondered if I really had the nerve to venture closer. Prancer wanted to move, so I made my decision and headed in the direction of that intriguing slice of land.

It was deceivingly long, that half circle of beach, dunes, and rock-edged shore. Mary was right, I needed to watch my step. After about fifteen minutes of steady walking, we reached an area that put us in plain view of and from the white house. It looked like the kind of place where one's grandparents might live. The windows were large and sparkling, and the chimney offered a steady stream of white smoke; an aroma of fruitwood filled the air. It reminded me of when my dad smoked a pipe filled with a cherry tobacco mix.

I came upon a flat rock and sat down, Prancer at my feet. I kept looking at the house, which was still about a football field's length away from us. I watched the gulls dip and glide, and I tasted the salt on my lips as the waves tirelessly rolled in then retreated. It was the most magnificent show on earth. I looked back toward the house and at that moment Prancer stood and looked in the same direction. I was stunned to see the figure of a man – tall, lean, wearing a tan jacket and jeans. I couldn't tell if he was wearing glasses, but it was evident that he was looking our way. Prancer gave a soft bark and tugged on his leash.

"Stay, Prancer. Sit," I insisted as I stood, my heart pounding. We were all like statues. Prancer sat, but then he stood again, his chest forward, his legs positioned to run. My heart broke. He wanted to go to his master. I'd grown to love this creature, but in truth his love for me was less than the love he'd been denied for the past year.

"Wait, Prancer," I said to the dog, my eyes on the man. From my coat pocket, I took a small notepad, a pen, and two paperclips, and scratched a note: *He's missed you.* I added my name and phone number then wound the paper around Prancer's brown leather collar, fastening it in place with the paperclips. The tears flowed and my throat constricted as I unfastened the leash. I watched as Prancer ran; he stopped to look back at me briefly then turned and bounded off to the man he longed for.

I watched long enough to see the two embrace as old friends, and when I could watch no longer, I turned, and as fast as I could walked back to the motel. I gathered my things together then saw Prancer's food bowls and a ball. Salty tears streamed down onto my jacket as I placed them into my travel bag and headed for the ferry.

On Sunday I was miserable. I'd planned to still be on the island, but now I was back in Prides Crossing alone. I'd missed former boyfriends, and even some relatives, less than I was missing Prancer. By seven that night, I'd cried until my eyes were swollen and red. I was glad for Finn and Prancer, but that didn't stop the pain of missing that hairy dog. I needed to get out of the house. I called a friend and invited myself over for coffee, a glass of wine, anything. When I got back home at ten-thirty, there was a message on my machine: "Hi. Thank you for the wonderful gift. When you come out this way again, please come by. I make the best clam chowder anywhere. I would welcome the company."

I sank into a chair by the phone and cried more than I ever dreamed I might. When I could cry no more, almost ill with a self-induced headache, I listened to the message again, then wrote down the number from my caller ID.

*****

Thanksgiving was celebrated. Molly and my mom hit it off as I expected. Everyone enjoyed Molly's four-inch-high cheesecake, but I was glad when the festivities came and went. No one, including Molly, inquired about Prancer's absence; they must have thought it appropriate for me to leave him at home.

The weekend following, I thought about Woods Hole and the ferry. Not this time – I couldn't stand the thought of making the trip without my sweet companion, and I wondered if he missed me at all.

Chapter Three

Over the next week, I focused on articles requested by Bill. My mind during work hours was occupied with an anthropology-related article as well as political controversies and events thriving throughout the city and state. Sometimes I longed for those days studying the finer points of journalism, when I questioned, but loved, my youthful lust for the imagined word. I stole time for writing poems, writing a short story here and there, sketching trees around the university, inserting creativity with the absolute truth and trials of life. Now I found myself working overtime then going home to an empty house where I most often curled into a ball on the sofa. I could still smell the soft essence of Prancer's beautiful body – I touched where he had chosen his own space; in just a few weeks, he had become part of me.

When the first weekend in December came, I felt the pressures of others' expectations nagging at me. There were two pre-holiday parties with people at work and in city hall. There were presents to buy – something for my parents who always claimed to need nothing, and then my older sister and her family: a husband, a four-year-old, and a seven-month-old baby. While my relationship with my mom was solid, it was evident that at twenty-eight, she expected me to be married with kids, like my sister who was three years my senior. I felt and understood the hope they all had that I would meet someone and settle down. It hadn't been in the cards.

I decided to escape it all and called Jim to arrange my trip to the Vineyard. I had no assumptions for the sentimental journey. I did not expect to see Prancer – it was a certainty that he was happy to be reunited with his good friend, but I found myself thinking about the cozy room at Jim and Mary's, the scallops, and a glass of good wine at The Watermark Café – maybe I'd walk where I could glance over at The Narrows and think about what to divulge to Bill. The entire subject was complicated. I had no idea and was desperate to avoid thinking about what had happened to cause the plane crash and for Finn to be hiding out in an undisclosed space.

The wind on the Vineyard was abrupt and cold, the dampness from the sea accentuating the penetrating chill. Arriving at the motel, I gathered my coat closer to my body, clasping the collar to my throat. Before turning the key in the lock, I turned to look at the sea, its green-blue waves capped with white, never ending in their quest to claim the island. It made me feel small and unimportant in the stream of life, so vulnerable, while the sea was alive with an unending exuberance.

My eyes turned to the sky, the gulls swirling above, at least eight of them in their continual search for food. How uncertain was their next meal I wondered and made a mental note that tomorrow I would buy a few loaves of bread for them. Not particularly nutritious fare, but filling until they found what they needed to stay strong.

In my room I choked back tears as I walked toward the sofa where Prancer had rested his head. I questioned my sanity in having taken the journey at all – what had I expected to gain? I answered my thoughts with the truth – I was looking for closeness. I wanted to be near to Prancer, to catch even a glance of him, and I felt compelled to discover more about Geoff Flynn. Geoff – Granger. Flynn – Finnegan. My pulse beat faster.

With my coat still on, I walked to the hot plate and began heating water for a cup of coffee. Two muffins sat on my table and I smiled noting that one of them was chocolate chip. Mary and Jim were like having two noninterfering parents looking after my needs. I broke off a small piece of the chocolate chip muffin and popped it into my mouth as I waited for the water to boil. I walked to the front window and looked out to the rocks and the sea, the gray sky tossing lighter gray clouds around as if rearranging clothes in a closet. I'd been so happy here with Prancer, and now I wasn't happy anywhere.

With the coffee cup in my hands, I moved to the sofa and sat down. I placed the steaming brew on a small table then unfastened my coat and slipped my arms out of it. Then I pulled it back over my shoulders and stared at what I could see of the sky from where I sat. Wherever I had chosen to be on this weekend, Pride's Crossing or the Vineyard, I would be trying to recover from losing Prancer.

Before I even finished asking myself the question about having set him free to run, I stopped myself with the truth – Prancer was not meant for me. His heart was with another; he'd endured the loss long enough. I was behaving as my parents had raised me to be, ethical, but it felt miserable.

Finishing the last sip of warm coffee, I slid my arms back into the coat sleeves and walked to the car, retrieving my laptop computer and a bag of pretzels. Back inside, I flipped open the computer and turned it on, then ran myself a hot bath. In the tub filled with lavender suds, I nearly fell asleep, then noticed the water cooling. I pulled the drain and dried myself before slipping into casual slacks and a navy blue sweater. Bare feet were covered with warm socks, a small Thanksgiving gift from my mother.

At the computer, I stared at the dancing design against a blue screen then tapped a few buttons inviting myself into the world of Granger Finnegan. When his

close to you

name popped up, I stared at it for a few minutes. I started to read his name, just his name, when I covered my eyes with my right hand and murmured out loud, "Oh, my God, can I do this? Can I dig into this man's life more than I already have? Why am I unable to let go? He's alive. I know he's alive. And he has my dog."

I placed my hands together and stared at the screen, feeling that I was an intruder, feeling frightened for why I felt compelled to investigate further. This was a man who had obviously been betrayed by a woman and her boyfriend – he had an accident. Or was it an accident that no one but me understands he survived? That's Granger Finnegan over there on The Narrows, it must be, it is; there can't be a question. And what do I do with this information? I can't tell Jim and Mary. I can't tell my family. And I certainly can't tell Bill. He'd definitely want to bring the information forward, exposing Granger Finnegan to whatever he was hiding from.

I thought about closing the computer down then decided to search for anything new, just in case someone else was aware of the present situation. Was I really the only one who knew that this man was alive and keeping quiet?

When I had walked my fingers all over the keyboard in search of something I may have missed about this well-respected surgeon from Boston, it was evident that what was there in front of me, much of what I had written one year ago, was the same – nothing new. A vanished life, questions with no answers. I closed the computer and slipped my feet into shoes then put on my coat and gloves. I drove to The Watermark Café, ordered fried clams and white wine, then sat staring out to the dunes. I felt numb, locked in by what I knew and what I didn't know for certain.

As my meal was delivered, I'm sure I stared as Geoff Flynn walked in the door. He glanced my way then accepted a small table near the entrance. When I dared to look up from my plate again, he was studying the menu, a glass of wine in his left hand. I couldn't help but notice the long, slender fingers and thought how skilled he must have been as a neurosurgeon. Here on the island, he was unavailable to people he might have saved, and, in turn, he was saving wild birds.

By the time his meal arrived, I was nearly finished with mine. I wondered how to handle this. I would need to walk past him on my way out. Not that he should know me; there was no way he could have seen my face from the distance when I released Prancer to his care. I stood quietly having paid my bill, then walked slowly by him and out to my rental car. Turning the key in the ignition, I closed my eyes for a moment and took a deep breath as his features haunted me. They were strong, an angular face, his body lean and tall. I shook my head as I started the engine, scolding myself for allowing interest in the man to enter my mind.

close to you

On Sunday, I knew my day on the island would be short – it was a chore getting back to Pride's Crossing from my sea escape. Mary and Jim must certainly have wondered what I was running from, yet they never questioned my presence in their motel.

With a muffin in my hand and the loaves of bread I'd purchased the evening before, I sat on a rock formation just outside the motel and tossed half pieces of bread into the air, delighting the gulls who came in a flock of at least thirty. I laughed at their antics and marveled at their dives, then I noticed Prancer at my feet. I dropped what I had left of the bread and found myself stunned as the dog woofed at me slightly, evoking a response from his once upon a time friend. Tears streamed down my face as I hugged him close and told him how much I loved him. After several minutes, I looked toward The Narrows to see Geoff Flynn standing there, a football field away. Prancer turned to look at him, then he looked back at me. More than I could take, I hugged him again and then urged him back to his home. "Go," I half-heartedly demanded. "Go, Prancer – I love you."

The dog looked at me with his soulful brown eyes then with one last nudge to my leg, he turned and ran toward The Narrows. My heart felt shattered yet saved; this creature had turned me into a pile of mush.

When he reached Granger, I watched as the dog and man embraced then they both turned to look my way. I turned away, brushing tears from my eyes, making a hasty retreat back into the motel room. I gathered my possessions together, washed my coffee mug, and set it to dry, tidied the room and my bed, then left as quickly as possible. It was just after one o'clock. I'd be back in Pride's Crossing by four-thirty or five. And then what? The endless, dispirited emotions would envelope me – I was feeling hollow.

Escaping questions about Prancer's absence this time, I knew there would need to be answers for Jim and Mary at some point. I decided to tell family and friends that Prancer was with his original owner and leave it at that. I would eventually explain to Molly Penniman.

The drive home from the ferry was without joy. Having seen Prancer, having had the chance to embrace him, knowing that he remembered our companionship, was both wonderful and excruciating. While once there had been a sense of contentment going to my own small abode at the end of a day, it was now the loneliest place in the world. It was going to be horrendous explaining where Prancer was when I could not reveal the truth, except to Molly. She would understand, and she would be glad.

Exhausted with my emotional frailties, I knew I couldn't face Molly just then – I would seek out a time good for us to share what I thought and what I knew. She would become my conspirator in this complicated hope that someone she cared for was still alive and reunited with his cherished pet.

At my desk the next morning, Bill walked over to me with a short paragraph he'd written up regarding Granger Finnegan. My heart skipped a beat as I read that the disappearance added to the presumption, the much-loved doctor had died in the crash. I read it again, my eyes clouded, then handed it back to Bill.

"This was your story," he said. "Do you want to write it up in your own words?"

I shook my head. "No, what you've written is good."

He turned to walk away when I called to him. "Bill, what if there's more eventually? What if someone comes along with new information, someone like a neighbor or something? Could we reopen the subject?"

Bill gave me a long glance. "Sure, why not? I have my doubts that will happen, but you never know. We'll see. By the way, how's that dog of yours?"

I held back tears and smiled. "He's fine."

Chapter Four

As Bill walked away, I covered my face with my hands for a moment, then fearing one of my fellow reporters would see me and ask what was wrong, I moved my fingers to the keyboard in front of me and allowed them to rest there as I collected my thoughts. I had undeniably lied to Bill concerning this story. It was the last thing I would choose to do; Bill deserved the truth. I took a few deep breaths with my eyes closed then walked to the coffee machine. Hot and black, I took a sip then returned to my swivel chair and my responsibility to write about a Boston politician. That woman deserved my best efforts, but my mind was elsewhere.

My mother called that evening and invited me to celebrate my nephew's birthday with them on the weekend. Guilt-ridden, I promised to drop a gift off at my sister's house, but the weekend involved business. To some extent, I wasn't fabricating the time, but I led my family to believe that I had no choice. As a side remark before concluding our conversation, my mother inquired about Prancer. "You haven't mentioned that dog of yours lately. Do you still have him?"

My parents were never the animal advocates that I'd turned out to be and her voice reflected curiosity more than concern. "Actually, no. We found the original owner and Prancer is with him now." As soon as I spoke the words, I swallowed back tears and was grateful to hear my mother say, "Oh, well it's probably for the best."

Where had I come from? My married sister had no pets; my mother wasn't enthusiastic about having a cat or dog, yet I longed for the soft fur and personalities of these tender creatures.

When the call ended, I sat back and felt warm tears trickle down my face. I didn't brush them away. They stayed as the sweet memories of Prancer filled my thoughts. There would be another pet someday, I was certain, but not yet.

I washed my face and heated a cup of coffee, then decided to give Derek Halstrom a quick call. His wife answered, and I explained who I was. When Derek came to the phone, I felt a connection to this man who may have known Granger Finnegan better than most. His voice was steady, calm but with an air of curiosity.

"Hi, Cara. What's up? Anything new?"

I hesitated then began. "I was thinking about the crash, Granger's crash. You know that plane well; do you think there's the slightest chance he could have survived? I keep thinking he might have had time to eject before the plane went down. Am I wrong?"

Derek's deep breath was easily distinguished. "I don't know, Cara. I hoped so from the beginning, but it's been a year."

"But would he have had time to get out if he knew the plane had an issue?"

Again Derek drew a deep breath. "I'm guessing here, but yeah, I think if he had a warning that he wasn't going to be able to keep the plane in the air, he could have calculated a jump before going into the sea – again, just a guess."

I closed my eyes for a moment, the phone in both hands. When I opened them, Derek was speaking again. "You know, the nose on the Swift tends to be heavy, if he was going down, he'd know that it would be head first; I could see Finn making a last minute escape. He was exceptionally capable with piloting as well as swimming. I've nursed that theory, that he was okay someplace, maybe being looked after by a gorgeous mermaid or something. He was my best friend, Cara. I'm not the same."

I felt the tears slip down onto my lips again. I wasn't the same either, and I'd never met him.

"You okay? How's Prancer by the way?"

I couldn't say I'd given him away, and neither could I admit the truth. "He's great," I answered, then thanked Derek for taking my call.

"Anytime," he said. "Listen, if you ever hear

anything about Finn, please let me know. I don't care if it was discovered he's in a place being taken care of, hurt from the accident, unable to speak, anything. I'd be there for him. He was one of those rare individuals who made life better, not just in the operating room. You know what I mean?"

Yes, I understood what Derek Halstrom was saying. And when the call ended, I wondered if he knew more than he was letting on. Molly's message, the one with what she thought was Finn's voice, about the house for rent, could that have simply been a coincidence? The timing seemed odd. Maybe Derek was still in touch with his old friend after all.

I sat holding the phone as if it was a link to the missing man and his dog. Never had a story become so personally important. I'd always known I was quietly searching for more meaning to life than most people I knew. The disappearance of Granger Finnegan had gripped me from the first report on the TV news about his crash. I'd become invested in his loss and then the hope that followed. No body had been found despite an extensive search. Maybe, just maybe, he hadn't died. Now here I was, fairly certain that the man on the Vineyard with Prancer was Granger Finnegan. I could not comprehend my emotions – they were getting in the way of my life in general, even to the point that I was not honest with my mother about my weekend plans.

I sipped my cooled coffee then dialed the number

for Molly Penniman. When she picked up I asked, "Molly, are you going to be around this Friday afternoon late?"

"Sure," the woman said. "Can I interest you in a light supper?"

I laughed, "Peanut butter toast and tea?"

"Now that's a secret, but I just might throw a meatloaf or something in the oven, toss in a baked potato or two. I can have a little something for Prancer, too."

This would be the hard part. "Don't fuss, Molly; I love peanut butter toast. I just feel the need to talk with you."

"You okay?" she asked with a concerned tone.

"Yes. I'll see you Friday, maybe around four."

When Friday came, I felt a measure of release that I'd be able to level with Molly. She would understand everything I intended to reveal: the conversation with Derek Halstrom, the sightings on the Vineyard, the heart-tug of letting Prancer go to someone he seemed to know and adore. Molly would keep this information without sharing – I could trust her with the burden of suspicion as well as the personal loss of my wonderful pet; it would allow me to reason aloud, to share the grief with another person.

*****

Over a delicious meal of meatloaf, baked potatoes,

and creamed corn, Molly and I were quiet. I'd told her the details. I explained where Prancer was. When dinner was finished, we had hot tea in the rose-peony cups and she stared at me over a plate of sugar cookies I'd bought at a store on my way over.

"Have one," she insisted. "You look like you could use a bit of sugar."

I accepted a cookie and held it. After a few moments, I took a small bite and put the cookie down on my plate.

"So you think this man is Finn. And Prancer ran to him?"

I nodded. "I believe it's him, Molly. Otherwise I'd never have let Prancer go. I can't tell another soul about this. If it is Finn, it means that he's hiding out on the Vineyard, away from his home, away from his practice, away from some danger perhaps."

Molly took a sip of tea then placed the cup back on its saucer. "I get it. What I don't get is that he hasn't contacted anyone. What could be going on with Finn?"

"I don't know. I'm not sure how to find out either. I live my life thinking about this. I'm not one-hundred percent sure this is him, and yet, the man looks like the photos I've seen, and Prancer was alerted to him the first time I took him to the island. We were a distance from where Finn lives, if it is Finn, of course. But I trust Prancer's instincts. You should have seen him; he was ready to run the moment he and I caught a glimpse of the man more than a football field away, out on the rocks tossing food to the gulls. It was like he'd seen an apparition. It gave me chills along with a hefty heartache."

Molly nodded. "I can imagine. The fact that Prancer came back to bestow a greeting the last time you were out there…that's something truly special. I'll tell you, Cara, that's one smart creature – smarter than many humans I know."

I smiled. "Smarter than many I know as well."

We sat in silence again. I picked up the cookie and in three small bites consumed it all. Molly was right, I needed the sugar. She poured more hot tea and we sat staring out the window, dark with early evening.

"What are your plans? You have this secret you have shared with me, but you can't really tell too many people – if Finn is hiding out, we wouldn't want to reveal his whereabouts."

"I'm telling no one but you. You're the only person I can breathe easy with – this is about Finn's life, protecting him from disclosure."

"Not even your family knows?"

I took a deep breath and looked Molly squarely in her lovely brown eyes, almost the color of amber. "No way. My parents would insist that I owed it to my editor to tell him every detail. I can't do that. It troubles me immensely to deceive Bill, he so deserves my loyalty. But what if this situation is dangerous, what if Finn's life has been threatened, and by whom?"

Molly placed her cup down on its saucer and leaned forward. "I agree with you. I'll keep this to myself, Cara; you don't need to worry. It makes me think that the night I had that call about the whereabouts of the dog, it very well could have been, probably was, Finn. It sounded like him. I remember a time when he was at the hospital a few years ago. He had tried to call his dad to say he'd be late getting home. He couldn't reach his father. In fact, the poor man had taken a fall which has led to him being in a nursing home now. He was brilliant, an avid reader. But after that fall, it was never the same. Little by little, his deterioration became noticeable."

"The condition became worse?"

"Oh, yes. Finn took him into Boston where they tried a few procedures, but the brain swelling was a real problem. Then Finn brought Eve into the picture, trying to be kind to her and her daughter. She and George, Finn's father, didn't like one another. He'd lost some abilities, but he wasn't stupid. He pegged that woman as taking advantage of his son."

"Did he talk about her with you?"

"Once in a while, yes. He'd go out in the back yard and putter about with Prancer at his heels. If he saw me, he was quick to call my name and we'd chat over the fence. He made perfect sense in what he was thinking at first, but he began to be very forgetful – he'd even forget my name."

I thought how difficult that must have been for Finn. "So he'd lost his mother and then watched as his father faded."

"Exactly. Finn came home at night and helped his father take a shower, fed him dinner as his hands became weaker. It was sad to watch. He ended up in this place on the Cape that specialized in brain injuries. Finn felt bad to take him so far from Wellesley but thought it was the right form of care. He went often to visit, of course Eve never knew. He told me he flew into Hyannis airport, rented a car, then would spend a couple of hours with his dad.

"Poor man, I wonder if he's still alive. If he is, thank goodness he doesn't know about Finn. He'd be devastated. Losing his young wife was nearly enough to take him down. Except for Granger, I'm not sure George would have made it through that loss. He adored that woman."

I looked from Molly's sincerely saddened face to the dark beyond the windows. "It seems that family has had more than enough grief."

"Yes, they have. And to think Finn became a respected surgeon through all this turmoil. He's a valuable sort, Cara. I remember one time when he was maybe twelve, possibly thirteen, he found a little gray and white kitten in the yard. Finn came to me and asked if it was mine. I said no. He took it to several neighbors;

close to you

no one claimed the kitten. He came back to me with it and wondered if I would keep it until he asked his father, and at that time his grandfather as well, if they could keep it. I took the kitten and put it in the bathroom until I heard back from Finn. He did some fast talking, but he managed to convince his father and grandfather to let him keep it. It was a male, and Finn named it Lincoln after his favorite president. That cat lived through Finn's internship, had a nice long life with lots of love and good care."

I smiled thinking of the boy who had a heart for animals. "Did they ever find out where it came from?"

Molly smiled and took a sip of her tea. "They never found out; it has been a well-kept secret."

"What's the secret? Wait, did you have something to do with this little cat?"

"Me?" she asked with a tell-tale smirk. "I knew that boy needed more than two men in his life. At his age, something to care for was a good thing. In fact, he told me years later that having Lincoln made him realize he wanted to be a doctor. So, how about that? I may have been instrumental in his career. I've loved that boy from the moment I met him."

"He never discovered that you were the gifter?"

"Not yet."

When the evening was over with Molly, I felt a massive sense of relief to have shared my secret with her. She was understanding and sensible, and she would do nothing to endanger her beloved Finn.

I drove toward the Cape, a good two hours on a Friday evening, then stayed at a motel near the ferry. I felt drawn to the island, to the place where my heart wandered and wanted to be. I thought I might see Prancer again, yet I wasn't so sure I wanted that union. Seeing him, holding him, shattered my heart; his spirit was alive with affection.

Having been there once before without him, and grateful that I had not encountered either Jim or Mary, I wondered how I would explain Prancer's absence if they inquired about his whereabouts.

When morning came, I walked toward the ferry office, bought a round trip ticket, then stood in line before boarding. I felt someone's eyes observing me as I sipped a hot coffee and watched the rolling waves. Not my usual course of action, I turned to see who it was. A young man, probably a bit younger than my twenty-eight years smiled as my eyes met his. He carried a guitar case and an ample duffle bag. I returned a brief smile then turned back to the sea. Within moments, he was at my side, dropping his duffle bag and placing his guitar case at his feet.

"It never gets old," he said, his eyes to the white-capped waves and then to me.

I nodded. "It's pretty amazing."

"Are you visiting the island or do you live there?"

"I'm visiting."

"Ah, nice. I grew up on the Vineyard. Now I'm a traveling musician, just heading home for a week or two. Mom's cooking, rest – I'm ready."

I looked at him and smiled, noting his dark blue eyes. I could envision him on stage, thrilling a teen mob.

As the ferry pulled closer to the docks, he slipped the guitar case strap over his left shoulder, retrieved the duffle bag in his right hand, told me it had been nice meeting me, and left. I watched him go, half dragging the duffle bag, and thought how easy it was to pass a few words with a total stranger. I'd never been a highly social person. Two or three friends, never cared much for parties, and I didn't appreciate foolish behavior. Even as a young teen; I questioned how much fun I was. Maybe being a little less serious would lighten me up. Wished I'd asked him his name – maybe I could have gone to one of his concerts sometime. I thought about the mob scene which might have followed him and his fellow musicians. No, I wouldn't enjoy that so much – I really was party-deficient.

Without seeing Jim, I rented a car then made my way to the motel. Mary and Jim were both in the office as I walked in.

"Hey," Jim said with a big smile, "good to see you again, Cara. We're going to make an islander out of you yet. Where's that nice dog of yours?"

I swallowed back what I had rehearsed to say, then

without hesitation or a reply from me, Jim continued, "The seagull guy has a dog like yours. Saw him walking the pretty fella just this afternoon."

I felt obvious with my hesitation in response to Jim's information and found myself in a deceitful position. "Prancer has taken a shine to a dear friend – they need one another just now."

Jim shook his head. "Well, that must be hard. There was a definite bond between the two of you."

"I still see him," I said with sincerity and forced myself to slightly smile.

With the key to my unit in hand, and a sense of sorrow for somewhat deceiving Jim and Mary, I told them I'd see them later and couldn't get out of their office fast enough. I hesitated outside at the closed door and took a deep breath. Maybe this was going to be harder than I'd planned. Every thought of Prancer was a stab in my heart – Yes, I saw him, playing on The Narrows as though his life had been restored. I walked to the car, started the engine, and headed for my room. Inside I looked around and realized how lonely it was, but, then, it was lonely everywhere. I sat down on the sofa with my coat still wrapped around me then decided to come alive with a hot cup of coffee. As usual, a muffin, blueberry this time, sat near the little hot plate area. I broke off the sugared top and stuffed it into my mouth. I thought about going to the Watermark Café later – that decision could wait.

close to you

I drank my coffee, noted that the sun was forcing itself through the dense clouds, then decided maybe I'd just take a quick nap before a walk in the cold. It was wilting, all this deceit and solitary existence. I considered that when I returned to work on Monday, I'd find time during the week to visit Molly Penniman again. Suddenly her peanut butter toast sounded good, along with a dose of truth. I could talk openly with her about Granger Finnegan and Prancer. She would understand my actions. My family would have said I could get another dog.

Chapter Five

When I woke from the long nap I apparently needed, I looked at the clock on the wall. It was nearly four in the afternoon – I'd managed to spend my time sleeping rather than walking. It was already getting dark; seeing Prancer would have to wait until tomorrow.

I poured the half cup of coffee down the drain and ran a hot bath. The water felt soothing as I slid my body deeper, knees toward the ceiling. When completely dry, wrapped in a large towel, I decided on warm clothes. Light wool slacks and a brilliant red sweater, a gift from my sister last Christmas.

At just before six, I drove to The Watermark Café and hesitated – the dark blue station wagon I'd seen driven by Granger Finnegan was there. Did I dare walk into that congested space where my eyes were bound to search for a familiar face? I wasn't sure and sat in my warm vehicle for at least five minutes before turning the engine off and leaving the car. I walked directly to the door, pulled it open, and found myself face to face with Granger Finnegan. His eyes traveled my face and then there was the hint of a smile as he excused himself

close to you

and left the restaurant. My heart pounded as the hostess directed me to a small table, possibly the one just vacated by the doctor. I ordered wine and my choice of food then sat there staring out at the darkness. On a napkin, I began to make a Christmas gift list. A pair of warm sweaters and gloves for each one of my parents, a cozy blanket for my sister and her husband, and toys for the kids. I would pick up something for Molly, too. And maybe little thank you gifts for Jim and Mary. I loved Christmas, but this year was going to be punishing. I would need to fake my way through merriment, wishing for more, wishing for Prancer. He'd made a vast contribution to my life while leaving a vacancy in my heart. I wanted him back. I couldn't have him back – I understood all while feeling the loss.

The short drive back to my room after dinner was bleak. It was dark and cold both outside and in. Suddenly the thought of living alone depressed me, love escaping my life. It could happen; I'd known people who lived that way, with nothing to take care of except a clogged kitchen sink. I wanted more. I thought about past relationships – no one had what I hoped for: the ethics, the morality, the simple expectations in life.

After hanging my coat in the narrow closet, I sank into the softness of the sofa and switched on TV. I thought as I mindlessly listened to the news about what I'd do in the morning. I hoped for a walk where I might catch a glimpse of Prancer. And I found myself thinking more about Granger Finnegan. With many attributes as a surgeon and a neighbor, what could possibly have occurred to make him disappear from a full and prosperous life? I found myself wanting to console him, wanting to save him, but from what? Frustrated with my seemingly empty existence as well as the complex story behind his disappearance, I found myself exhausted. I fell asleep sitting up on the sofa, surprised to find Sunday's sunlight in my eyes.

After changing clothes, I walked to the edge of the motel's property, the chilled air at my throat, the gulls overhead. I looked over toward The Narrows and saw only the house and the land reaching toward the persistent sea. I turned and walked toward the office where I knew a good cup of coffee and a muffin would be waiting. Later, I walked longer than planned and found myself closer to where Prancer now lived.

Still there was no sign of him or his companion. I eased away, not wanting to be discovered nearby – I made my way over rocks toward the street and eventually back to my room where I packed and decided to leave on an early afternoon ferry. Why had I tortured myself with this destination when I could have stayed closer to Boston for needed Christmas shopping? I began to feel like an addict, harboring a craving for seeing both Prancer and Granger. I tried to analyze why the attraction to someone I had never met, to someone with a complicated existence.

I left the island having not seen Prancer. I wondered if it had been for the best – I wasn't sure what I'd do if he came bounding over the rocks to me again.

*****

Monday night after work I decided not to go back to Prides Crossing until I'd found at least a few gifts for my family. With Christmas just two weeks away, it would be a duty shopping trip. A list in my hands, I entered one department store and bought everything I'd intended. On the way out, I saw a section for pet supplies and toys. Without further thought, I bought a red and orange ball for Prancer and a small package of his favorite treats. I wasn't certain I'd see him before Christmas, or ever again, but the instinct to buy him a gift was strong.

It was near eight when I called Molly Penniman. She picked up immediately and asked where I was.

"Still in Boston," I answered. "Just finished a little Christmas shopping."

"You're lucky," she said. "I send a check to my son and his family – not exactly holiday fun, but it's a muddle when we live such a distance apart."

"I understand," I said.

"When are you coming for a visit?"

I smiled and looked down at my feet, packages in my hand. "I've been thinking about a visit soon. What would work for you?"

"What about tomorrow night? I need a good meal and if you're coming I'll cook. Do you like chicken potpie?"

"That sounds really wonderful."

"Good, then it's settled," she said.

Timing was arranged and I drove back to Prides Crossing thinking about all I wanted to tell Molly. She was the only person with whom I could be completely honest.

In my own quiet dwelling, I left packages on the entry room floor and hung my coat. The place was chilly and it was still. I looked around as I turned the heat up and lights on, thinking how wonderful it had been to arrive home to Prancer. I thought about getting another pet, a cat, a dog, even a guinea pig or two. I was mourning Prancer and accepted that reality. I did not want to burden another creature with my sorrow – I needed to be in good thinking form before I adopted from the local shelter. I reasoned that an animal should not be responsible for consoling me – I needed to be ready.

My day at work on Tuesday was busy; there were three short pieces Bill had asked me to write, each of them requiring sources for accuracy. They were time-consuming reports. My sense of guilt in not leveling with Bill was high; I felt caught in an emotional trap where I knew I was wrong as well as right. Bill wouldn't have kept the suspicions of Granger's existence quiet. He was a decent man, yet a leading national newspaper editor with the intention of informing his readers. Had he known about the likelihood of the doctor's probable life on the island, he might even have assigned the story to another reporter. I couldn't risk that happening.

After work, I called Molly to tell her I was on my way – it would be about an hour's travel time. I found myself anxious to see her, to enjoy the warmth of her home as well as the thoughts of consuming chicken potpie, something I hadn't had in months.

"You look like you're freezing out there," she said at the front door. "Come in, hang your coat, and follow me to the kitchen. Everything's hot and ready."

The aroma filling the house was wonderful – it reminded me of when we'd gone to my grandmother's where home-baked bread waited along with strawberry jam and butter. I missed those times and felt grateful for this newfound friendship.

"So any new sighting of our dog? If he were here, I bet he'd love some of this potpie," she said as salad, warm rolls and mashed potatoes were placed on her small kitchen table.

I took a sip of water then placed the glass down. "I went out this past weekend – came face-to-face with Granger, I'm certain. But no reunion with Prancer this time." With tears in my eyes I stopped talking.

With a respectful silence between us, Molly just

looked at me.

"I felt like it was Finn, that Prancer knew it was, and I couldn't keep them apart any longer."

Again there was a silence for a few long moments before Molly replied, "It must have been heart-wrenching for you to let that dog go – I know you loved him from the first moment. But he's reunited with his master, his first friend."

I smoothed tears away and stared at my plate.

"Fill that thing up," Molly suggested. "You look thinner every time I see you. Don't you eat?" She scooped mashed potato onto my plate and advised that I might try a bit of salad as well as the potpie.

"Letting Prancer run to him was the most uncertain act I've been responsible for – I wasn't sure, Molly. I trusted Prancer to know who this was, and their greeting to one another was like something out of a fairy tale."

"Will you go back out there in hopes of seeing him again?"

Again the tears flowed. "Yes, I even bought Prancer a ball last night. I envision him wagging that gorgeous tail, and of course, I know I'll cry when we part."

"By golly," she said, "you're braver than me. I knew the day I gave Prancer to you that I was doing the right thing, but this business of thinking it was Finn on the island, well, that took gumption. Eat your dinner before it gets cold. I think you did the right thing."

close to you

Dinner was delicious. Tea and ginger cookies followed as we sat in Molly's living room where a fire contributed warmth and charm.

"What's next?" she asked. "What are the big Christmas plans?"

I placed my teacup down on a side table and smiled. "I just did all of my Christmas shopping. In fact," I said as I stood and walked to my purse, "I have a little something for you."

Molly grimaced and complained that she had nothing for me, she hadn't been shopping. I told her this evening's wonderful meal was my gift.

"Well, if you take some home with you, that will make me happy. Now what did you spend your hard-earned money on for me?"

I smiled as she opened it immediately, no waiting for Christmas. Carefully, she unwrapped a silk scarf, decorated in peonies. She looked at me with glistening eyes. "You know, it's been years since I've had a gift this dear to me. A son doesn't often think of these things, but my husband did. He knew my weakness for these gorgeous blooms. Thank you. This is a spectacular gift."

"Do you have plans for Christmas day? I could pick you up as we did at Thanksgiving. My mother loved having you; the entire family would be thrilled to see you again."

Molly leaned back in her swivel rocker and smiled.

"Since my husband passed, I've elected to spend Christmas alone. He loved that holiday more than anyone I knew. I choose to get through the day by making myself some scrambled eggs, his favorite, and coffee. I decorate one of my ceiling-high plants with little white lights, and later I have a tuna fish sandwich and pumpkin pie."

I smiled at Molly's detailed account. "We have all the fixings for a great dinner; you'd be more than welcome."

"I appreciate your thought, Dear, but I'm steadfast in my decision. Your family was very welcoming at Thanksgiving, yet Christmas is different – I need that quiet day to reflect on a wonderful companion. I was lucky."

Letting the subject rest, we spoke about projects at *The Journal*, about articles I'd written that Molly had read.

I offered to get us each another cup of tea, and she let me. While walking into the kitchen, I thought about how relaxed I felt. Keeping Granger Finnegan and Prancer to myself had been crumbling my soul – I had so needed this wonderful woman's understanding as I shared what I perceived as the truth.

My drive back to Prides Crossing was long and dark. With the small casserole dish filled with potpie and mashed potato at my side, I thought of the leisurely evening. I had hoped for this sort of relationship with my mom over the years, but she was a director of life – my possibilities and adventures were more often scrunched than promoted. As much as I loved my family, I had the feeling that they thought of me as dependent, that I should never have left home at the tender age of twenty-two. I smiled at knowing that I had always felt capable and anxious to explore my own little universe on my own, for at least a while. My little house, my job where I had a by-line in a respected newspaper, and a couple of go-no-where romances had all been my own responsibility, with or without continual joy. As I drove past the sign for my town, I thought how Prancer had added to my life, yet I was resistant to another pet so soon. I would find love, one way or another.

*****

Closer to Christmas I had thought about spending a weekend on the island. I decided it might be dismal, cold, and alone where I had once been happy with a wonderful dog. I thought about Molly, how she chose to spend the holiday on her own terms, with a tuna fish sandwich. She was perfectly capable of cooking a wonderful meal, yet she wanted the sandwich. I understood.

After much thought, I reasoned it might be best for me to stay in the city, near to family festivities. Then I remembered the ball and the snacks for Prancer. He might not know it was Christmas, but I did. Suddenly it became essential that I go to Martha's Vineyard once before the holiday. I would take cookies to Jim and Mary, and I would have seafood at The Watermark Café. I would find a way to get the ball and snacks to Prancer.

Perhaps I'd be brave enough to make a phone call to accept that island invitation.

Chapter Six

Arriving at my motel room on the Vineyard was emotionally troubling – I loved being there, yet I scolded myself for not recovering from Prancer's absence. Over a cup of hot instant coffee, I sat down and questioned my ability to get on with life. Was I suffering the forfeiture of the dog or was the stress something deeper? Perhaps my concern for Granger Finnegan? I had always been a logical, free thinker, yet here I was, questioning where I should be, what I should believe, and how to proceed.

I emptied my cup of coffee into the tiny kitchen sink and changed into clothing suitable for The Watermark. I would eat my sentiments – I would have scallops with a glass of Riesling. Tomorrow I would take a long walk, cold or not, and I would find a way to leave the little gifts for Prancer. I would toss them into his yard if nothing else. But what if I was seen through one of those pretty old windows in his new home? Or was the home really new to Prancer? Perhaps the home was familiar, as was the owner.

With the gifts in the front seat of my car, I drove to

the restaurant. It was early in the day, almost four and getting dark. I loved Christmas but wished it was spring. I wasn't prepared for darkened days and swift winds cutting through the fabric of my coat. Nor was I prepared for merriment with family and office parties. Everything was incompatible this year – I felt divided and conflicted concerning my life.

I pulled up to the almost empty parking lot, hesitated, then shut off my engine and walked into the warm space filled with the aroma of fried clams, wide-cut French fries, and home baked rolls with butter. I'd had nothing to eat since this time the day before – I was ready for my plate of scallops.

Told to sit wherever I liked, I chose a back corner where I could see the entrance as well as swaying sea grass blowing in the light from the nearby building. There was something healing about the island. I wasn't sure, maybe it could be just any island, but this one had a spiritual strength. You could almost promise yourself that everything was going to be all right.

Before a dozen or so others entered and were seated, I had consumed my meal and was ready to go. Back in the car, I shivered against the dense cold, turned the heater to high, then sat there testing my own resolve. Would I now go and toss this gift to Prancer so that daylight could not catch me? Yes, that was the best idea I'd had in a while – I would park near the house on The Narrows and I'd hurl the small package as close as

I could. Prancer, with his gumshoe nose, would certainly find his present and Granger Finnegan would be none the wiser. I decided not to further intrude, even by phone, on the life Prancer now lived.

With one assertive throw, the package landed in a pathway to the house. I was proud of my athletic abilities, which had never been much of anything. Prancer would find the gift. That was all that mattered.

Back in my room, the darkness of that Saturday one week before Christmas, I called my mother. Everything was set for Christmas day – the dinner, the festivities, all centered around my sister, Lisa, and her family. I understood the significance of making the day work for children, yet I longed for something different. I wasn't sure what, but church on Christmas Eve, coffee and sweet rolls for Christmas breakfast, then a few hours to make sure everything on the table was perfect for a Christmas feast seemed shallow this year. I questioned myself. Was I being self-centered? And just how bad was it to own that sentiment? I simply wanted more, or perhaps something different, something that I could not identify. The more I considered the coming week, the more I decided on escaping some of the traditions – I would, instead of going to one of the office parties, share another visit with Molly Penniman. She was a kindred soul.

*****

Sunday morning was a gift. I looked outside to see what appeared to be diamonds softly floating from the sky. Snow, sparkling from brilliant sunshine, drifted past my windows, and I felt my smile being met with tears. I was lonely. That was everything and anything at that moment, perhaps at that level of my life. I had achieved success, more than I had expected, with the newspaper. It had become a dream job, one I'd worked hard to secure. I had known romance, two relationships I thought had promise until they didn't. It had taken a dog to fill the space that was now hollow in me – thoughts of Prancer finding his gift made me whisk away the tears. I needed a push, something else to make me realize that I had promise, not only for my work but also for my longing to find a relationship that mattered, be it with a two-legged or four-legged companion.

Not sure of what I would do with the day, I knew that it would not be spent inside the motel room. I dressed for the cold, packed my few belongings, then drove to the motel office to say goodbye and Merry Christmas to Mary and Jim. I left them with a package of cookies from a famous Boston bakery, told them I'd be back soon, perhaps when the weather was warmer.

"There's a package here for you," Mary said as she retrieved a gift from beneath her desk. "It was left at the door."

I looked at the box wrapped in red foiled paper, tied with a length of simple string, a six-inch piece of evergreen tucked into the center. It held a tag with my name, Cara, and that was all.

I glanced at Mary and at Jim who stood to the side and half behind her, both of them looking as curious as I felt and must have appeared.

"You don't know where this came from?"

"No idea whatsoever," Jim said. "Found it at the door this morning."

I thought about opening the present, then I held it and felt myself trembling with wondering who left it and what was inside. Without opening it, I again wished my friends a wonderful holiday and went to the car. Near the ferry docks, I left the vehicle at Jim's rental stand, walked to the ferry with my bag, and found a seat after purchasing a cup of coffee. I could not bring myself to open the present. I held it close to me as my eyes traveled the intensely intoxicating green sea, the waves fighting the sides of the ship, the motion of the vessel determined to win. Back on land I called Molly.

"I'm heading toward home from another weekend on the island," I explained, and realized I no longer could claim Prides Crossing as home. The truth was I felt as though I wasn't secure in home being anywhere. "I was wondering if you're busy today. I thought it might be nice to see you again before Christmas."

"Come along," she encouraged. "I'm in the middle of making an apple pie. It was my husband's favorite for any holiday treat. If you don't share it with me, I'll eat the whole damn thing myself and gain twenty pounds. Come, I'll make something for dinner."

I laughed at the thought of an apple pie being consumed all week by one person. "Sure. But let me bring dinner. There's a place not far from you where the Italian food is superior. Do you like eggplant parmesan? They make the best I've ever had."

"Bring it on," Molly said. "I might as well plop a few more pounds on this old body. What do you think, a couple of hours?"

I looked at my watch. I'd just left Woods Hole from the ferry; it was after noon. I told her I estimated two hours, maybe two and a half with stopping for the food.

"Sounds perfect. I'll finish making the pie and then maybe I'll dust."

"Don't dust for me," I said with laughter. "I'm used to that stuff."

My drive north-west was one in which I avoided thinking about the mysterious package. I wanted to reveal the contents but felt caught up in fear of the unknown.

When I stopped for the food, I noticed an array of sweets on a bake table. A box containing colorful fruit renditions in marzipan caught my eye – I had one wrapped for Molly, another token for the season, her hospitality, and her friendship.

Pulling into her circular driveway my eyes went to the Finnegan home: dark, without a sign of Christmas, still for rent. Molly's door was embraced by a handsome swag made from a variety of green boughs, a sumptuous red bow at its crest. I was about to knock when Molly opened the door and smiled as she lifted the bag of food from my hands and ordered me inside.

"Holy smoke," she said. "How many people did you think would join us? This must contain food for a week."

I stepped inside to the aroma of a wood fire and willingly left my coat across a chair in the hallway. It felt more than right to be in that house – heart-wrenchingly not so in the home of my parents. I did nothing to make them happy it seemed. I was not so much of a church-goer; I wasn't married, and my relationship with my sister, while agreeable, felt disconnected. I had never felt that we understood one another. I regretted that lack of emotion.

"Come in and tell me what you've been up to. Out on the island again?"

Molly placed the bag of food on her counter and began to unwrap the contents. Her table was elegantly set with her peony patterned dishes, tea was steaming in the pot, and the apple pie sat at one end, ready to be sliced and served.

"Come sit; let's eat while it's hot. This stuff smells divine. Did it come from Da Vinci's?"

"You know the place?" I asked as I took my seat, unwrapping warm rolls.

Molly nodded. "You bet I do. It was Finn's favorite. He often brought me their meatballs or a sub. He knew my love of Italian food."

Chills enveloped my body as Molly sat across from me. There was no way to escape thoughts of Granger Finnegan when everything seemed to lead me directly to him. Of course what did I expect when I kept returning to his next-door neighbor's home and to the island where he now lived?

"Did you see Prancer this time? Anything else new?"

I scooped some eggplant and sauce onto my plate, selected a small roll and butter, then watched as Molly poured a red wine into two elegant glasses.

"No, I didn't see him. Work and the Vineyard; nothing exciting, but all is well. How about you? Have you heard from your son and his family?"

Molly grimaced. "Not yet. He's a last-minute type. I'll hear from him, probably on Christmas Eve. I'm fine with that though; he's a busy man. Tell me about you. I know there's more to your life than work and going to an island in the dead of winter."

I took a sip of wine then a bite of my food. I swallowed and looked up at Molly. "I've been thinking about my life," I said. "Everything is totally ordered. I work at *The Journal*, and I love it. Newspaper writing is in me, delivering information and stories to others holds a huge satisfaction. Writing in general pleases me –

someday, maybe a novel – we'll see. But for now, I'm a little discombobulated."

"Whoa," Molly began, "that's a word I haven't heard in a while. What's missing from your life? Everything okay at home?"

"Everything is okay. I really have no complaints; it's just a realization that I'm running a bit on empty at the moment. You know, when you're in college, have the prospect for a great job on a nationally respected newspaper, and have a boyfriend who seems to have the spark, life holds promise. Now, well, I'm so settled. I have a job I do pretty well – the subjects of my writing are interesting, and I have this adorable little cottage I rent in a charming setting. But…"

Molly looked up at me. "But?"

I smiled, shrugged, and continued to devour the eggplant drenched in delicious sauce.

"Oh, I brought you something," I said as I slipped out of my chair and retrieved the marzipan. I placed it down next to Molly's plate.

"I don't know if you like this. It was a favorite of my grandmother's. I always love how they fashion almonds and sugar into these adorable fruit motifs."

Molly leaned forward and looked at the box. "Like it? I love it. Marzipan is a favorite of mine; my own parents always had it in the house for holidays. Thank you, Cara; this is wonderful."

We sat back, licking our lips, sipping wine, sipping

hot tea, and staring at the pie that we were both too full to do more than smell.

"You haven't mentioned Finn," she said as she placed her teaspoon back on the saucer.

I shrugged. "Nothing new really; I don't know what to make of it. I keep trying to convince myself that it's him on the island with Prancer, but every once in a while I have this creeping doubt."

"Why the doubt? You've seen him at close range, haven't you? Does this man look like Finn?"

I looked around the room then back at Molly. "Yes."

"Then it's Finn. I'm telling you, Cara, there's something very odd that transpired between him and that Eve. That woman was not his type, not in any way."

"What type did he go for? Did you know any of his lady friends?"

Molly nodded. "I met a couple. There was a cute little girl in high school, kind of a cheerleader type, although I don't know if she was into that at all. Blonde, pretty and perky, you know the type. He took her to the prom – pictures were taken in the doorway of the Finnegan house. Then there was Irene. She was while he was in college, a singer with the Boston Symphony. Neither of them seemed to ring his bell, but he was popular with the girls, a very classic sort of fellow. I miss him."

"He's close to forty now, right?"

"Just about. He's a catch, which makes me wonder all the time what he was doing with Eve."

I sat back in my chair with the warm teacup embraced in my hands. Finn and I seemed to have missed the proverbial boat with romance.

"Something strange happened today as I was checking out at the motel."

Molly looked at me as if waiting for me to continue.

"Someone left a package for me at the office. It was wrapped with my name on it."

"What? Now that's strange. What was inside?"

I shook my head. "I don't know. It's still in my car."

"Oh, for God's sake, go get it. Let's see what it is."

I stood slowly and then walked to my car without a coat. The air was biting cold, and I hurried back inside with the wrapped gift. I set it on the table and nearly laughed as Molly and I stared at it as if it was an uninvited crocodile.

"That looks like Finn's handwriting. Open it," she demanded good-naturedly.

With slow hesitation, I untied the string and moved the piece of greenery to the table. I unwrapped the red foil as though dismantling a bomb. Lifting the cover to the box, I found a pair of warm gloves in gray wool. A note accompanied them; *Thank you and Merry Christmas* – it was signed with a paw print.

I looked at Molly then placed the box and note before her. She looked at the package contents a long time. Her eyes met mine as she said, "Why would Finn give you a gift?"

I shook my head. "I have no idea."

Molly continued to look at my face as if expecting a more conclusive answer.

"I tossed a couple of things in the path of his house for Prancer."

"What? When?"

"Yesterday, when it was dark. I left a little toy and a favorite dog snack."

Molly smiled and sat back in her chair. "There's no 'just' with that confession. To Finn you made a wonderful gesture thinking about his dog. I can't see how that man is anyone else but our Finn, Cara."

Soon after, we wished each other a merry Christmas, embraced, and then parted.

Driving back to Prides Crossing was tiring. I'd had a long day and felt ready for a bath and warm pajamas. With two assignments lined up for the next day, I gave each some thought and decided to nudge my computer for additional information. The thought of the gloves crept into my mind. I tried them on and found them perfect, soft and snug. I looked at the note again, so typical for a doctor to write close to an illegible scrawl. I smiled, then placed them back into the box and set them aside.

On Christmas Eve as I wrapped a few gifts for family, the phone rang and I heard Molly's voice. "Cara, I had a surprise gift that arrived about an hour ago, and couldn't wait to tell you."

"What was the gift? And from whom?"

"It was a gorgeous plant, with white and pink Poinsettias. They're my favorites this time of year, and were always a gift every year from Granger Finnegan."

Chills ran through my body. "Any card, name, or message?"

"Nothing, but it could be from no other. Finn always knew I loved the white and pink. He gave me a plant like this every year over the past fifteen years or so. That man on the island, Cara, there's no question."

When our call ended with each of us wishing the other a wonderful Christmas, I sank into a small recliner and kicked up the footrest. Feeling wilted, I thought about how guilty I felt for keeping this information to myself. Bill would have been excited to know that Granger Finnegan was alive. He would have wanted a crew of people to cover the story, with photos of his island habitat and numerous, invasive questions. Like Bill, the journalistic endeavor existed within; still I could not divulge the intrigue associated with the well-known surgeon. No matter what happened, I would not be the one to reveal Granger Finnegan's new life.

Chapter Seven

Christmas Day turned out to be consoling. The food and family were exactly as we'd planned, with my parents' neighbors stopping in to have a glass of my dad's potent eggnog and a slice of my mom's more potent rum cake. Merriment abounded and I felt guilty for having dreaded it. The drive back to my own place was pleasant – I listened to Christmas carols along well-tended roads, clear even though there had been a coating of snow.

With assignments on my mind, I adjusted to the time away from the island. I decided I was crucifying myself by going there, by watching for signs of Prancer and Granger. I had let them consume me and all I'd gained was frustration and a deeper sense of loneliness. Determined to sink deeper into my work, I found myself exhausted at the end of the day, prepared to surrender personal thoughts to sleep.

In mid-January I called Molly to check in. Her voice sounded low, congested. "Are you okay?"

"Getting over a dang cold," she complained good-naturedly. "Otherwise, yes, I'm okay."

"Could I bring you some food? How about some minestrone from Da Vinci's?"

"You're very kind, but no. In fact, my son called again last week and when he discovered I had this miserable cold, he had all sorts of frozen foods sent to me. I've got enough for a family of twenty. But thank you, Cara; I appreciate the offer. Any more on Finn? Have you been to the island?"

I took a deep breath. "No, I've been preoccupied with work, and it's pretty cold out there just now. Maybe in a month or two."

Molly was silent for a few moments then asked, "Does it make you feel worse being so close to Prancer and not having him with you?"

I sank into my sofa and tried to conceal my sigh. "It's a combination of things, I guess. This time of year is not especially inviting out there, but to some extent I suppose I need to admit that I miss my pal. He made quite an impression on me."

"Love is like that. It lingers, it settles in. It hasn't been that long, Dear. You'll be okay."

I held the phone and wondered.

"When I'm clear of this rotten cold and cough, I'll give you a call. We need a peanut butter toast supper soon."

I smiled. "Sounds perfect."

Turning the phone off, I held it for a few moments. I thought of Finn and Prancer then slipped my hands into the gloves I'd left on my coffee table. There I sat, looking at the gloves and wondering how Finn and Prancer were managing on the winter-quiet island. On impulse, I called Jim and Mary to say hello and to see how their holidays were. They were fine and assured me that Christmas was merry – filled with family, gifts, and an abundance of delicious foods. They encouraged a visit soon – the island was hushed, many of the stores were closed, but The Watermark Café was open and good as ever. I believed them and felt the urge to go there sooner than I'd planned.

*****

Two weeks later I drove to Molly's for our casual supper of toast with peanut butter and my choice of homemade preserves, raspberry or peach. I chose raspberry and decided it was the ideal accompaniment to oozing peanut butter on warm toast. It had been quite a find for me to meet and become friends with Molly Penniman. Our conversations were interesting and light, as though we'd been friends for a lifetime. There was absolutely no reason for any sort of deception. I'd been slightly dishonest with my parents at times – they often chose to console me with their suggestions for a better way to handle my world. Molly let me think of what to do, her approval was reassuring as well as comforting. Maybe, I thought, that's how parents are, overinvolved with their children's choices. I learned in my early twenties to keep much to myself, to pretend all was well when there were times I felt emotionally tangled. While my family was kind and instructive, I didn't always choose their route.

A month after visiting Molly, I decided a trip to the Vineyard was due. It was early March, still cold with snow on the ground, but spring was near, and I could envision the cozy motel room and a delicious meal of scallops or clams. Nothing tasted quite as good as island food. I made my arrangements for the ferry and headed there on Friday afternoon.

Jim and Mary had my room freshly cleaned, the heat was up and warm, and a chocolate chip muffin was waiting in my kitchenette. I took a deep breath and smiled at the familiarity of the space and the view of The Narrows from the front window. I hadn't realized how much I'd missed being there – everything seemed to welcome me back.

With no hesitation, I sank into my soft bed, pulled the covers closer, and thought how much I needed this diversion. I thought about Finn and Prancer and wondered what they were doing at that moment – were they out walking or inside with a glowing hearth?

Early Saturday morning I felt ready to make my bed and pull on some warm clothes. I walked to the window overlooking the sea, allowing my eyes to scan the shoreline. I glanced over at the home on The Narrows. There was no sign of man or dog, and I found myself fearful that they might have left. Slipping into my coat and wearing the gray gloves I'd been gifted, I walked outside and looked in both directions along the coast. Then I saw Prancer, his beautiful body glimmering in the sun as he jumped to catch what might have been a tossed stick. I smiled as I watched his playful moves and then he suddenly turned and stopped as he stared in my direction. He turned toward the man as if for permission, then galloped toward where I stood. I could not believe that after several weeks, he remembered and came to me, hurtling rocks and dunes to greet me. With tears streaming from my eyes, he landed in my arms, his back feet on the ground, forepaws at my shoulders. I hugged him with a fierceness I had not known I possessed. I wanted to keep him with me forever. I looked around Prancer's beautiful face toward the man who waited, hands stuffed into trouser pockets. "I love you so much," I whispered as Prancer's brown eyes focused on my face. "So very much, Prancer." When I looked up toward The Narrows, the man stood looking our way and I supposed he wondered if I'd reclaimed his dog.

"You need to go, baby, but come to see me again. I love you, Prancer."

As though he understood every word, he turned to face his friend and then with one last glance to me, bounded back toward The Narrows where he danced around the person who ruffled the soft ears. Again an object, perhaps a stick, was tossed in the air and precisely caught by Prancer. I could see that he was healthy and happy, which gave me great pleasure. I watched them for a few moments then turned away, forcing myself to look in the opposite direction. I took a step backwards and headed toward my warm room. With car keys in my hand, I decided a ride toward Edgartown might offer an opportunity to focus on something other than my own sense of oneness.

In the town's center, I found a bookstore open and wandered inside to browse. I left there with three purchases – one on the island's history, and two novels. I walked next door to a small bakery and bought myself a vanilla cupcake with strawberry icing and a cup of coffee. Sitting in the car with my treats, I thought about how the island was waking up from its winter sleep. Little shops that had been closed over the barren months were now bristling with anticipation of tourists and the island's occupants. It was all a renewal of life, spring emerging.

On Sunday, I decided dinner at The Watermark would be around three then I would turn in my car and board the ferry. I felt better, rejuvenated by this visit, or was it the delicious cupcake? I smiled at my own foolish thoughts and began to think about the articles I'd be tackling first thing Monday morning. Then I thought about where I was with Bill. I felt completely remorseful about not telling him the truth, yet my allegiance to Granger Finnegan's existence could possibly be life altering if I revealed more.

At just after three, I pulled into the Watermark's parking lot near to the door. As I did, a dark blue car pulled up next to me, and I watched as Granger Finnegan, not noticing me, walked into the café. I sat stunned by the coincidence, then put my car in reverse and headed toward the ferry. All the way back to Prides Crossing, I thought about the new finds in my life, Molly, Finn, Prancer. What in the world had I thought about before I knew of them?

Pulling into my driveway I turned off the engine and took a deep breath. I was hungry having had no dinner at The Watermark Café. I went into my house, shrugged off my coat, and opened the refrigerator to see what possibilities lingered there. Grilled cheese and tomato would be supper. I prepared it, ate it with hot tea then opened my computer to get started on tomorrow's projects. My need to escape personal thoughts and concerns was relieved with work. A little after nine, I called my parents and spoke with my father. I did not mention I'd just come from the Vineyard – he would have asked why I was there in this dead time of year. I didn't think of March as dead, just waiting to wake up with jonquils and crocuses, robins and golden finches. I thought of March as a new-born, waiting to cast joy on the land with its colorful offerings and lingering sun. My conversation with him was pleasant – they'd been to visit my sister and also an elderly aunt. My family was composed of good people even though at times I found them restricting. Maybe I was the weird one. That thought made me smile.

I worked for another two hours before shutting the computer down and changing into pajamas and warm socks. I watched the eleven o'clock news then turned off a few lights, always leaving one on in the living room and another tiny light in my bedroom. Crawling beneath the covers of a warm quilt, I thought about what was closest to my heart – Prancer, Molly, Finn. They had become first in my emotional storage unit, and in some ways I felt guilty for thinking of their welfare before anyone else's. I started to question why I felt slightly removed from everything and everyone I'd known in my life, why had this disappearance of Granger Finnegan so affected me? His vanishing had led to a treasured friendship with Molly Penniman, a crushing devotion to a large dog, and Finn. I decided in the semi-darkness of my room that I needed to stop thinking about them; I needed to sleep. Before I closed my eyes, I said my version of a prayer: *Thank you for introducing me to Molly, Prancer, and Granger Finnegan.*

Chapter Eight

Over the next few days my workload was overflowing. An article on a disgraced politician took me to four separate interviews and hours of deciphering what was actual and what was fabricated. It took a while to sort out who was dependable and who was simply searching for media attention. That happened more frequently than I would have preferred. I worked late day after day, going back to my Prides Crossing home in the dark after eight o'clock.

One evening as I walked in the door I heard the phone ringing. The caller ID indicated that it was Molly, and I picked it up quickly.

"Did you hear anything about Eve?" she asked with anxiety in her voice.

"Eve Finnegan? No, what's happened?"

"Well," Molly began, "it's the strangest thing. One of my neighbors is a nurse at the Glinwood Hospital. She said Eve was brought in a few nights ago, battered and bruised from an automobile accident. She saw her briefly, but Eve wasn't her patient. She had no idea what happened. You didn't hear anything?"

close to you

I sat down with my coat still on and felt numb. "No, nothing. What about her little girl, was she hurt?"

"Apparently the child wasn't with her. I was hoping you could dig into this a bit and see what happened. My neighbor was reluctant to tell me anything more – you know, the privacy factor and all."

I slipped out of the coat and sat there on my sofa, stunned with this information. "So you don't know how serious Eve's condition is?"

"No, nothing. I tried to ask a few simple questions, but my neighbor, while sympathetic to my curiosity, was not revealing anything more."

"I need to go in that direction tomorrow – I'll stop at the hospital to see if I can find out more about Eve, and I'm curious about Jill's whereabouts."

"If you find anything out, give me a call. Not that I had any feelings of affection for Eve, but I wouldn't wish this sort of problem on anyone, and especially the child."

When our call ended, I sat statue still and thought about how unpredictable life was – moment to moment, everything could change.

The next day when I'd finished an interview in the area, I drove to Glinwood Hospital and inquired about Eve Finnegan. The woman at the desk looked puzzled then asked if I was looking for Eve Finnegan or perhaps another Eve. I explained the circumstances, and she told me there was a listing for a patient named Eve brought in through an accident, but the last name was not Finnegan. I hesitated, feeling confused, and wondered if Molly's neighbor had the wrong name, the wrong person.

The woman at the desk asked if I'd like the room number for a visit.

I must have looked startled. "She's approved for visitors, so you might want to check on her. People sometimes get admitted using another name, just to keep loved ones from worrying or for privacy reasons."

She gave me the room number and directions to the third floor. I thanked her but felt ambivalent about the visit. Then again, I had nothing to lose. If it wasn't Eve, I could phone Molly and tell her that there'd been a mistake, the patient was not the Eve we knew.

In the elevator, I had the uncanny feeling that I was walking into an unknown situation. At her room, I took a deep breath and walked in to see Eve's familiar face asleep, her face swollen with cuts and bruises. As my eyes focused on her fragile form, she opened her eyes and stared at me with questions in her expression.

"Hi," I managed to say softly. "I heard you'd been injured in an accident. How are you feeling?"

Eve looked at me for a few moments, and I wondered if she was unable to speak.

"I'm alright," she answered.

I moved closer to the bed and felt great sympathy for the pain she must certainly have suffered. "Is there

close to you

anything I can do? Is your daughter okay?"

Eve again looked at me with hesitation and then replied, "Jill is okay. She wasn't with us."

I wondered who she referred to with the word us. Then she added, "Tony was killed."

I felt a chill run through my body, my speech halted by astonishment. Eve looked at me, seeming to understand my loss for words.

"I'm sorry," I managed to say, although I wasn't accurate with my sentiments. I didn't know Tony – I had heard only negatives about his character. Eve was silent.

When I left her room and the hospital, I called a friend, Rob McCloud, on the police force to see if he could tell me more about what had happened.

"I can't divulge too much, Cara, but I can tell you it's public record. Eve was driving. They hit a tree – the guy was killed instantly."

I held the phone for a long time after that call. This was becoming a tangled, curious issue. I called Molly that evening and told her about the visit. I didn't mention Eve had been the driver, just that Tony had died. Neither of us was thrilled hearing about a death, but having no emotional investment in the man, we expressed shock more than sorrow.

"Did she say anything about Finn?"

"Nothing," I said. "I can't figure out if I like her or not. She's not a warm person, but she's been through a lot; a single mother of a child, a rowdy sort of boyfriend who is now out of the picture, and a missing husband. I'm not sure I know how to talk to her – she's been toughened by what seems to be a challenging life."

"That's accurate," Molly said. "When you put it like that, I feel a little guilty for being so hard on her. I mean, I never said anything mean to her, but I wasn't exactly cordial when she moved in with Finn. I was disappointed in his wife selection, and I suppose it showed."

I wasn't sure how to respond to Molly's words. Eve wasn't someone I'd wish to have in my life, but certainly she'd had her share of shattered illusions.

When our phone conversation ended, I sat down with a cup of tea and thought about the broken people in the world. It made me realize how lucky I was to have a fairly, if not a shade lonely, tranquil life. I had no struggle to contend with and couldn't imagine having to deal with Eve's sort of complexity. I wondered how much she'd cared for Tony.

In the morning, I woke with the idea that it might be nice for me to take Eve a small bouquet, a plant, something to gladden her existence. I wondered, too, who was caring for Jillian. At noon, I spent my lunch hour picking up a colorful plant and taking it to Eve. When I walked into her room she was just getting back into bed, moving slowly, then pulling the covers up to her chest. She glanced up and saw me, her expression blank.

"Hi," I began. "Thought a little color might help," I said as I placed the plant on her windowsill overlooking a parking lot and busy Boston landscape.

Her voice seemed frail when she thanked me, continuing to look like she wondered why I was there.

"Sit down," she said indicating a chair next to her bed.

I did as she suggested and we stared at one another. Out of dead silence, just as I was thinking I should leave, Eve asked if I'd heard any more about Finn.

There was nothing but lies in my soul regarding him – I could not tell her that I was almost positive he was alive on the Vineyard. I shook my head and told her I knew very little. She studied my face as though a bug was making its way around my eyes, my nose, my mouth – it felt awkward.

"We weren't married, you know."

Stunned with this revealing statement I was silent.

"It was all to give Jill a chance to recover, and who better to recover with than the surgeon who operated on her brain? There was no union. We lived in the same house, hardly even ate a meal together with Finn's schedule, but the masquerade was needed. His father wouldn't have wanted his reputable son to simply live with a woman, and the neighbors would have frowned at the situation as well. We claimed to be married – it worked."

At a loss for words, I said nothing. I know I stared at Eve's scarred face for several minutes. It was she who spoke, breaking the silence.

"I let Tony believe that Finn and I were a couple, solidly married. I didn't want him in Jill's life." She hesitated and looked out at the sky through the window three feet from her bed. Then she looked back at me. "Tony hated Finn. Finn was everything Tony wasn't. It caused a lot of tension when he decided I should get a divorce, take Finn for all I could get, and then go off with him to some sort of life in Chicago." Again she hesitated, looked at her hands and then folded them. "I didn't want Finn to get hurt. I was afraid he might, so I agreed to leave here and go with Tony. At least that's what I led him to believe."

"You weren't going with him?" I asked.

Eve shook her head. "Never. He was a mistake from the beginning. I wasn't sure how I'd escape him, but I knew I'd go back to Arizona, to my mother's. She had invited Jill and me to stay with her until I had a job and a place of my own."

I sat there diverting my eyes from her face to the window every few seconds.

"I hope," she began, "that Tony didn't cause Finn harm. I wouldn't put it past him. He actually went to the hanger where Finn's plane was stored to take a look at it. It gave me chills to think of him going there. It was just days later that Finn took off for the Vineyard –

he'd filed a flight report. Then everything ended, and Tony insisted I get out of the house. He wanted me to sell it. Of course, I couldn't since it wasn't mine to sell. He convinced me to at least rent it until Finn's will was settled. All of this renewal into Finn's accident and disappearance has had me on edge – I'm afraid Finn must have died in the crash, and yet, nothing of him was found."

My urge to tell her the truth was weak. I sympathized with the concealed life she'd known while having a sick child, but I could not reveal the possibility that Finn was alive. Knowing that they had never married, or even been in love, made it easier to be deceptive. I was quiet for several minutes and so was she.

"So, Jillian is with your mother in Arizona?"

Eve nodded. "I was just back here to settle a few things when Tony showed up, insisting we go for a drive."

"I should get going," I began as I stood, "but I can come back if there's anything at all that you need."

Her voice became softer as she thanked me, and as quickly and quietly as I could, I left her room. Outside her door, I leaned against a wall and closed my eyes for a moment. A nurse came along, and I was afraid she'd think I was ill, so I opened my eyes and started to walk.

No one said a word to me as I made my way to the parking lot and my car. Once there, I sat for a while before starting the engine. When I felt my strength flowing back into my veins and limbs, I decided to visit my police officer friend. Did he know that Eve was not married to Granger Finnegan? I needed to be careful about what I said – this could lead to a deeper investigation and expose what actually happened with the plane crash.

In a crisp, dark uniform, his badge gleaming from the overhead lights, I sat across from Rob as we sipped strong precinct coffee. "So, still on that Granger Finnegan story, huh?"

I looked at him and half smiled. "Barely. I'm hung up on the accident involving Eve and her companion. What caused it? Do you know?"

Rob spilled a bit of coffee from his cup onto his uniform and looked down at his abdomen as he brushed the liquid away. "Funny you should ask. We went over that incident a few times, checked the area, checked the speed situation. It was broad daylight, no rain, no reason to have an accident. She was driving – he was basically a sitting duck. We wondered, but we couldn't prove or disprove anything. With bigger fish to fry, the case was closed."

I took a few sips of coffee then stood, thanked Rob for his time, and left the coffee in a trash can on the way out. Sitting in my car for a few minutes, a solitary place to organize my thoughts, my reporter instincts came into play. Did Eve cause that accident on purpose? And if she did, could I blame her?

I started my engine and headed back to work. With a lengthy article to write and deliver by the end of the day, I forced my thoughts to focus until I could return home and clear my mind.

That evening, with yet another grilled cheese sandwich and an apple at my side, I thought about calling Molly. What would I say to her? I thought about Finn and wondered if he should know about Eve's accident. And how was I to accomplish that? I couldn't just call Finn or stop by his island home to tell him. Despite my feelings, he and I didn't know each other at all. I felt like the peanut butter between my two slices of bread, and with that thought, decided that yes, I needed to talk with Molly.

"Come on out," Molly urged at the other end of the phone.

"Well, not tonight; it's already after seven, but what about tomorrow night? I could probably be there by six."

"Sounds good to me. Anything new?"

"Yes, a bit, I'll tell you about it tomorrow night. May I bring something?"

"Do you want more than peanut butter toast and tea?"

I smiled as I held the phone and kicked off my shoes. "Not really. I love your peanut butter toast and tea. But I could bring a cake or something."

"Nah," Molly said. "Just show up. We'll rough it for tomorrow night."

With our call completed, I heard myself sigh and tried to relax. The tension from the deceit was getting to me – I was keeping secrets from Bill and now Eve, and then there was Finn. If Tony had been a threat to him, had caused his crash, it might make a huge difference to him – he might feel that he could return to his practice now that Tony was dead. My head was spinning – I couldn't wait to talk with Molly and hear her logical reasoning regarding Eve's accident and Tony's aggressive behavior.

I looked at my grilled cheese sandwich and decided it was cold and uninteresting. I tossed it outside for some animal to enjoy, put the apple back in the fruit basket, then heated myself some canned chicken noodle soup. The hot meal was probably not as nutritious as it could be, but the warmth felt right to my taste buds. Someday maybe I might actually try to learn to cook for myself – then again, maybe not.

All I could think about the next morning as I stopped for coffee before work was Eve and the accident. My instinct told me it had been intentional – maybe not to take Tony's life, but to at least injure him while she made her escape. I could give her the benefit of doubting it had been a planned end, a necessary one.

close to you

Chapter Nine

When I entered Molly's home for our planned meal, I caught the aroma of home-baked bread and something else I couldn't identify.

"I hope you like corn chowder," Molly said as we walked past her elegant dining area to the cozy kitchen with its copper pans suspended over a marble island.

"I love corn chowder. In fact, I could live on soup; I haven't had one I didn't like."

"Good to know," Molly said as she placed ladles of creamy chowder into shallow bowls. "My husband and I always liked soups; his favorite was French Onion, mine was a good split pea or tomato. Here, slice yourself some of this bread – I had the urge to bake for your coming. I do enjoy our visits, Cara."

I sat down and reached for an ornate bread knife, slicing enough for the two of us to enjoy with our chowder. "I love our visits, too. In fact, I need them. You're the only person I can talk to without fear of receiving a scowl."

Molly sat down across from me and began to butter a slice of her warm bread. "Now does this scowl come from someone in particular?"

I buttered a slice for myself and then left it down on my plate. "I don't want to sound like a complainer, but my parents are not always that understanding of my life. I think I knew from the time I was ten or eleven that I would need to be independent of them as soon as possible. They are very traditional people; you may have noticed that at Thanksgiving."

Molly smiled. "I did, but I was raised in that kind of house so it didn't affect me. I had an older brother who went to law school and became a prominent attorney. He was several years older than me. Being a girl and all, I suppose in their old-fashioned ways, they thought of me as someone's wife and momma. I did as well, but I also saw myself as a business woman."

I looked up from my first sip of delicious chowder to Molly's wonderful face. "So, what happened?"

Molly smiled. "I did more than I ever dreamed I would and nearly gave my parents an early demise. I went to business school in Boston, graduated with honors, and at the age of twenty-two, took a lead position in Dymo-Tech."

"Dymo-Tech here in Massachusetts?" I'd interviewed their CEO less than a year ago.

"That's the one. I was promoted after two years to a top executive, then to CEO. The company today is flourishing because of an advanced idea I came up with. Heads shook when fifty years ago a gal took the reins and put the company on the world map."

I was stunned. I had no idea that Molly had ever worked in a world of engineers and technical surroundings. I'd thought of her as comfortable in a beautiful home, not as a brilliant young woman making her mark in business.

"After I married and had my son, I left the tech world behind and started to draw on my other passion, painting. I had some success with that, too, and it satisfied my need to be present in this marvelous life. I've really had a ball, Cara."

I smiled at her before taking a bite from the still warm bread. "You amaze me. I never would have guessed."

"Surprised the heck out of my parents, too," she chuckled.

Joining her merriment, I replied, "I'm sure it did."

"So, now you understand why I get it when you speak of your parents being traditional. They look at your sister as being the normal one, married with children. You sought a career as a journalist – they probably thought that was risky, maybe even frivolous."

I laughed. "You're so right. They tried to talk me into becoming a nurse or a teacher. They were terribly disappointed when I didn't marry at twenty-three after a college boyfriend got down on one knee. He was a church-goer and had a decent job. That was the prize. I had to make my own way. And if it sounds like I don't love my family, that would be wrong. I do love them, and I know they love me as well. It's just that we have different visions."

Molly scooped some of her chowder with her spoon then looked up at me. "That's exactly what it is. Don't let it get you down – it's life, it's individuality, it's healthy. Keep them guessing." She intentionally and loudly slurped the soup. We both laughed until we had tears streaming down our cheeks.

The chowder was the best I'd ever tasted, and the homemade bread, with its dense quality and laden with butter, was outstanding.

"So," she began as she patted her mouth with a napkin, "what's going on?"

I left my spoon in the empty bowl, took a sip of tea, then looked at Molly. "First, this was delicious. Thank you, Molly. I can tell you fussed with this great meal."

"It's not over," she winked. "I made a little batch of cookies. We'll have some with more tea after you fill me in. I could tell by your voice last night that you were stressed."

I looked out into the dark and then back at Molly's face. "It's about Eve. I had two visits with her, just to check in, and well, to get a little more understanding of the accident. Turns out she was driving; her passenger was Tony. He didn't make it. Eve will be okay with some time and rest, and Jillian is actually in Arizona with Eve's mom, but the bombshell she dropped is this, she and Finn were not married."

Molly's face turned to stone.

"They agreed to pretend to be married so that Jill's father would back off. Eve didn't want him in her daughter's life, and the other factor was Jill's surgery. Finn was eager to see her through recovery, to insure that the procedure had been successful. He was being kind to them – there was no real marriage."

Molly took a swallow of tea then looked me in the eyes. "You mean they were never a couple? They did this for the child's sake?"

I nodded.

"And Eve told you this?"

"Yes. She was very matter of fact about revealing the truth. I think she simply wants to recover then get back to Arizona where her mother is waiting to assist her with a temporary place to live. She's not someone I'd find myself sitting down with the way you and I are, but it seems she's had a hard life with some wrong moves. She's ready to make a change."

"Good grief!" Molly began. "Every one of us – Finn's father, his friends, neighbors – we all thought they'd married. Now that I think of it, I don't think the term married had ever been mentioned. Finn noted that they were a couple, a family. I suppose we all took it for granted that he'd married that girl; so much for jumping to conclusions."

I looked away again, toward Finn's house which was barely visible.

"So what's the next move? Will you tell Finn about Eve's accident? He probably doesn't know anything about it. She thinks he's dead, right?"

I looked back at Molly and swallowed some warm tea. "I suppose he knows nothing of this. It's not like it was written up in the papers or anything since she isn't a prominent person. But I have no plans to tell him. I don't know how I'd approach him. I haven't ever spoken to him. And what if that isn't Finn out on the island with Prancer?"

Molly half smiled. "Cara, I think we know it's Finn." She hesitated as she studied my face then continued. "You know what I think? I think you've found yourself in love with more than just Finn's dog."

A surge of adrenalin flowed through my body as I stared at Molly. No, surely not anything as dramatic as love; interest maybe, a devotion to the truth perhaps, but not love. I sat there thinking that this concept was ridiculous.

"No, Molly, no."

Molly's eyes focused on mine. "I'm not going to sit here and argue the point, but I think you're in denial, Cara. I've thought from the time I first met you, when you took that dear dog and invited him into your car and your life, ultimately restoring his life, that you were going to be something special to this case. You're

close to you

enmeshed in my dear friend's trauma. I know you didn't plan on this, but I do think you've managed to fall in love with a man you've come to know through other sources."

I sat back in my chair feeling drained. I'd admitted to myself from the beginning that I was invested in this case, that it was more than a story about someone who went missing. Yet I'd never considered loving this man, a being I'd never met. I'd questioned my deep interest, I'd wondered why the mystery stayed with me and why I didn't want to dig it up again, like a corpse I might discover had really died. I didn't want Granger Finnegan to be dead. I looked up at Molly then finished my tea. She poured me more and I stared at the beautiful peony cup.

"Not trying to make this into something it isn't," she said, "but there's every reason for you to think of being Finn's saving factor – you could be the one who tells him it's safe to come home. You're his type."

I smiled at Molly. "Really? Why do you think of me as his type? This is a lot like a very strange blind date. I don't know, Molly. I've wondered myself why I felt attached to this story, to this man. After reading all the charitable things he's done over the years, it was hard not to find ample amounts of respect for his profession and his spirit. Is that love or simply admiration?"

Molly shook her head. "Good love has all that: respect for the person, deserved admiration."

I picked up my cup of hot tea and took a sip as I stared again into the darkness. I wasn't sure what I was feeling, but my bet was that the last thing on Granger Finnegan's mind was romance. If Tony had been a threat, or if he'd cut the fuel lines in Finn's plane, Finn's mind was probably on survival.

Molly stood and walked to the stove, retrieving a plate of cookies which she set before me. "Have one," she said. "They're chewy ginger cookies, my mother's recipe."

Later that evening, while driving from Wellesley to Prides Crossing, a long, dark drive at night, I thought about Molly's suggestion, that maybe I was falling for Finn. Could she be right? I questioned her words – I questioned my emotions. I had found myself attached as never before to a story and its leading character – without the privilege of meeting him, I knew him. I wanted him to live forever, not sure at all that I could bear the agony of his confirmed death – it was easier for me to assume life and to get on with other articles.

I'd found throughout my twenty-eight years I'd felt deception and cruelty in many humans, yet I found more beings that were kind, good, worthy of praise. When I had the liberty of knowing them, I tried to make the account of them accurate. I wanted the readers of *The Journal* to know that person as I had through an intense interview.

When assigned the Granger Finnegan case more

close to you

than a year ago, I had the urge to beg off on that report, but I didn't. I walked into the story, meeting the beloved doctor through others' eyes. To be honest, I believe I began to feel more justified in doing so than I had with any other. I thought about a patient who asked the paper to help him thank the neurosurgeon for his renewal of life – he'd had no funds to pay for a surgery that would have been thousands of dollars and would have lost his home in paying for the needed remedy, so Finn had volunteered his efforts at no expense. Shamed by the media attention regarding the high cost of the procedure, the hospital set up a minimal payment plan to accompany Dr. Finnegan's pro bono deed. The article was a favorite that year – at least five years before his shattering wreckage in the waters off the Vineyard.

Thinking back to the interviews with his colleagues as well as former patients, Granger was a phenomenal human being – a man who took his oath to *do no harm* seriously. Everyone loved him, and now I wondered, is this what happened to me? Did I begin to fall in love with Granger Finnegan's spirit? The concept frightened me, and if this was actual, how did I not recognize this before Molly Penniman did?

The pull toward the island was magnetic – my mind felt scrambled with questions I thought might become more uncomplicated if I was at Jim's and Mary's motel by the sea. When the weekend approached, I made reservations for the ferry and found myself traveling a surging sea Friday night, coffee and an apple for my supper.

On route to the Vineyard, I stood at the rails of the ferry and watched the sun recede, as though the sea claimed the beauty of the night. Soon, I knew, the moon would cast its irresistible glow on the surface of the water, the land, its inhabitants. Nature was the eminent factor for all of life – a gift vastly unappreciated by those who would favor technology, drugs, and drink. I never understood how anyone read a book on a train, on a bus, on a ship. There was so much to observe, to appreciate for those moments or hours.

I tossed the core of the apple into a waste barrel then sipped the remainder of my cooled coffee. I thought about landing at the Vineyard. Jim had been contacted and a car reserved. I would drive to my room and then what? I thought about Molly and wondered if she'd say yes to an invitation to the island. She limped slightly at times; perhaps she wouldn't enjoy the journey, the ramps, and few stairs to travel on the ferry. Once there, in my rented car, in the motel and restaurant, I felt certain she'd be fine. I decided that the next time I saw her I would extend the invitation. I thought about the opportunity to point out The Narrows, the house, the dog, the man who might seriously be her dear friend.

Arriving at my room held an assortment of

close to you

emotions. My first internal rumbling came from thoughts of possibly seeing Prancer, and I laughed at myself for finding the importance in first seeing a dog. Not an ordinary dog, but one in which I had invested my heart. Then I felt the pang of doubt as I questioned my feelings for Granger Finnegan.

While I began to think Molly had a point, that perhaps I had fallen into the deep pit of caring for someone I knew only through my own investigations and interviews, I wondered how wrong or right that might be. Not in my years at *The Journal* had anything remotely like this situation occurred. It was the unraveling of Granger Finnegan's life that held me captive, that made my mind drift to him with the hope that he was alive. Suddenly, the prospect of him not existing became unthinkable; he had to be there in that lovely old house on the island's rocky shore. Who else would have drawn Prancer so willingly to his side?

I changed from office clothes to casual then headed without hesitation to The Watermark Café. I was starved and it was getting late, nearly eight when I left my room. Outside, my parka zipped up to my neck, I studied the moonlit clouds above and took a deep breath of mild air – spring was on its way and I was thrilled with the concept of being on the island when the jonquils there made a dazzling appearance in bursts of yellow.

The drive to the restaurant was brief, and I was glad

to see just a few vehicles parked there. To my relief, none of them resembled Granger Finnegan's dark blue station wagon. Once inside and seated at a small table overlooking the moonlit dunes, I ordered coffee and my usual choice of scallops. Again my thoughts turned to Molly, how much I thought she'd enjoy this place.

On Saturday morning I drove to Menemsha and parked my car near some of the fishing vessels, watching as lines were untangled, boats were secured or unfastened from the piers, seagulls circled with the hope of a free meal. This had been a favorite place for me as a child when I'd visited the island with my family. My father always bought quahogs there to make chowder, and he would buy me a freshly cooked clam cake. I found myself missing those days when being a child was secure and free of concerns.

My dad had been good at introducing my sister and me to new tastes, new adventures. While I loved the little jaunts and explorations my father instigated, my sister was reluctant. If there was a store where she could find a toy or, when she was a teen, a new pair of earrings, the island's exploration became valid. For me, it was the thrill of finding a new rock, a shell, sea glass on the shore, and digging clams in early morning light under my father's direction. Some of my thoughts made me feel sad, so much of that was gone once I journeyed off to college and never really went home again.

After walking around by the piers and breathing in

close to you

the salty air, I walked to a small café and bought myself a fresh clam cake and hot coffee. Having skipped my early morning muffin at Jim and Mary's, I was hungry for the food as well as the adventure.

Sitting at a small table, I watched the activities both inside and out, including the jovial fishermen claiming one over the other how large their catch had been. A good-looking young man with a head of dark hair gave me a wink and nodded just before his arm was seized by another man, old enough to be his father. I smiled as the gray-haired gentleman urged the younger one back to his boat.

When I left the café, I walked a bit through the village then purchased a postcard for my dad. I wrote on it the old and reliable words, *Wish you were here.* I addressed it to both of my parents – Mom had always been sensitive about being included.

The remainder of the day was spent browsing shops and meandering the beach where I found a beautiful piece of blue sea glass for my small collection. Before heading back to the motel room, I bought another coffee and just sat, loving the warmth drifting into my chilled body.

Before going out to dinner I called my family. My dad greeted me with a sense of joy at hearing my voice. "Where the heck are you?" he asked.

I smiled and told him the Vineyard. He made a comment about missing that place and thought he needed a trip there soon.

"You and Mom should have a weekend out here when the weather is nicer. I was in Menemsha today, remembering the times we bought quahogs and clam cakes – we had some great times."

My dad was silent at first then spoke softly. "Those were good days when you girls were little. I'm not sure we can recapture those times, but I sure would like to try. Do you still hunt for pretty shells and glass?"

I could feel tears flooding my eyes. "Yes, I found a piece of blue glass today. I think I need your help in finding more."

Again he was silent. I said his name and he responded weakly, "I'd like that a lot. I don't know why we stopped going there. I think because your sister was never a fan of the long trip to the Cape and then the ferry to the island. Your mother and I will have to plan a trip in May or June, before the tourist season. Gosh, those were wonderful times out there."

I knew my dad well enough to know he was probably brushing tears away and wondered where my mother was. Before I could ask, he told me that she was babysitting at my sister's home so that Lisa and her husband could see a Boston play. I took a long breath and remembered that my mom had always been an advocate for Boston culture, the museums, theater; I missed those times. Boston held opportunities for every possible source of entertainment and social enlightenment. I needed to get back to doing some of that – diversion from the island and Granger Finnegan at this point would be helpful.

On Sunday morning I had coffee and a muffin with Jim and Mary in their welcoming lobby. We talked about what I was working on at the newspaper, and I concluded by telling them that my parents might be coming to the island in a month or two. They offered them a suite and said how much they'd enjoy meeting my mom and dad.

I walked the shoreline as much as I could, wary as I chose my steps over rocks and masses of seaweed. At one point, I stooped to retrieve a golden shell and a piece of clear glass, smooth from the sea's insistence. I put them in my pocket then looked toward The Narrows. I saw no sign of man or dog and I asked the gulls, "Are they still there?" It would be an immense loss if I discovered they had gone to another location, even off the island.

At three, I boarded the ferry and watched as the exuberant sea and clouded sky became my companions traveling back to the mainland.

Chapter Ten

Shedding my jacket as I walked into my house, I looked around and wondered why I had not yet painted the walls I'd promised myself I'd do. The owners had given me permission more than three years ago, and here I was, still living with pale blue-gray. I walked to the kitchen and made tea then sat down on my sofa to appraise the situation. Yellow for the bedroom, soft tan for the living room would work, with red pillows against the dark brown sofa. I was responsible for cheering myself up. At the age of twenty-eight, surely I could conquer an upgrade in this small dwelling. I made a list to pick up paint and brushes to begin the transition.

Once I had exhausted that decision, I thought again of Granger and Prancer. Where were they? Could they simply have been inside the house or had they moved? Without knowing that Tony was no longer a threat, wouldn't he choose to stay in that beautiful location where seagulls cried for help? Yet maybe his plan was to move about, to evade a confrontation. For the first time I felt uneasy about not seeing them. I would go

close to you

again the following weekend, and this time, I would stay closer to The Narrows.

When I arrived home the next day after work my phone was ringing. I could see by the caller ID that it was Molly. I picked up the phone quickly, hoping all was well.

"Have you heard any more from Eve?" she asked.

I sat down leaving a bag with paint and brushes on the floor then unfastened my jacket. "No, have you heard something?"

"No, but I've been thinking a mile a minute. If that woman had anything to do with her boyfriend's death, who's to say she wouldn't have plotted and planned Finn's crash?"

I thought about the question for a moment then replied, "But what would she have to gain? If they weren't married, she'd have no right to his property."

"Think about it. She put a for rent sign on the house, and there were valuables. Finn's grandmother had a beautiful selection of pricy jewelry, and his grandfather had a valuable coin collection."

I closed my eyes for a moment and understood exactly what Molly was implying. Especially if Eve thought Finn was dead. Who would know what she took?

"I don't know, Molly. How would we even find out if she walked away with stolen goods? You're right though: if she took the Finnegan belongings, who would know except for Granger?"

We both were silent for a few moments before Molly said, "I don't trust that woman. I pity the little girl with her medical issues, but the mother is one of those people who takes advantage. I'm sure she wormed her way into living with Finn – he's soft-hearted enough to have pity on her situation – I'm just thankful he didn't marry the wench."

I laughed at the term wench, but I began to worry about how truthful Eve had been with me.

"Suppose she asked you about Finn just to see if you'd tell her anything? Maybe she's hoping he's gone so he wouldn't notice anything missing. I'm sorry if I sound doubtful of her actions, but she was not particularly likeable. Did you get to see Finn and your dog this past weekend?"

I took a deep breath. "No, I may have missed them; I took a ride to Menemsha and walked around there for a few hours. I looked toward their house several times without seeing either of them the entire weekend."

"You don't suppose they've moved on, do you?"

Again I took a deep breath. "I was told the house was bought with cash. I can't imagine Finn moving away and leaving that gorgeous old place."

We were both quiet again for several moments.

"This is a bit of a mess," Molly said. "We really have no idea what's going on. I so want Finn to be alive and well."

close to you

When our call ended, I sat with the phone in my hands and admitted to the same concern Molly expressed. What was Eve up to? If she had the ability to arrange for Tony's demise, even getting injured herself, could she have been the mastermind of Finn's crash? It was odd, too, that Jillian had been left with someone when the auto accident occurred. As conspiring as Eve might be, she certainly would not allow for an accident where her child was involved. My head was spinning. All I knew was that Eve was not to be trusted and her knowledge of Finn's whereabouts needed to remain unknown.

I thought again of Finn and Prancer not being in sight over the weekend. The weather had been nice, sunny and bright, no excuse to be inside. What if they had disappeared? What if I caused their departure?

With no knowledge of my motives, Granger Finnegan could conclude, having seen me at the motel grounds often, that I was an investigator, that should I discover his survival and whereabouts, I would divulge his existence. I scolded myself for thinking such negative thoughts – then I cried.

Several minutes later I dried my tears and warmed my cooled tea in the microwave. I drank it then chose a banana for supper. I ate stupidly, but that was nothing new. When I'd finished what served as a meal, I decided to begin painting my bedroom the sunny yellow I'd chosen, and I decided that tomorrow I would pay Eve another visit, providing she was still at the hospital.

Before leaving for work, I called to make sure she was still a patient at Glinwood. She was but had been scheduled to leave there that afternoon.

I spent three hours at my *Commonwealth Journal* desk, finished a report, then left word that I was going out for a possible investigation. The investigation part was authentic, the reason was left unsaid. I went to Glinwood, took the elevator to the third floor and Eve's room, and with her back to me, found her packing a suitcase.

Hearing my footsteps, she turned around with a startled expression. "Have you new information on Granger?"

"No." I shook my head and took a few more steps into the room. "I see you're preparing to go home, or to Arizona."

Eve hesitated. "Yes, to Arizona in a few days. I have unfinished business, but I'll be leaving soon."

When she turned toward me, I noticed a beautiful stone, what I felt sure was an Emerald, on a thick gold chain. She noticed that my eyes went to it and immediately covered the stone with one hand. "It's pretty, isn't it? It was a gift from Granger."

Something inside of me churned as I remembered what Molly had said, that Finn's grandmother had some valuable pieces of jewelry. "Yes, it's lovely. So, you're leaving today. Are you staying with a friend?"

Again she hesitated as though she might be tempted to ask what business it was of mine. Instead she half smiled. "Yes, a friend is picking me up this afternoon. I'll finish what I came here to do and, in a few days, goodbye to this nightmare."

I wasn't sure what she meant by nightmare – I wondered if she meant Finn's disappearance or her involvement in unsavory deeds.

"If I discover anything new regarding Dr. Finnegan, would you care to know?"

Eve stopped folding a pair of slacks into her suitcase and stared at me. "Yes, I suppose so." She gave me an address at Beacon Hill for the next few days, then her mother's address in Phoenix. I was surprised she'd been so free with that information, but then I thought about how motivated she might have felt for permission to go back to Wellesley for items she had hoped to take. I was angry with myself for not suspecting Eve before this, that Molly had thought this through as I should have done. I wrote the two addresses down and wished her good luck if I didn't see her again.

As soon as I was back in my car, I called Molly and described the necklace.

"That lovely emerald belonged to Finn's grandmother, Anne. She wore it often. A few nice pieces were given to Cynthia, Finn's mother, but the emerald was Anne's birthstone, and I doubt it would have been given away. Finn would not have done that, especially knowing he was going to be parting ways with Eve once Jill was well. I'm telling you, Cara, that woman has tricks up her sleeve."

Back at work I began to dig out information for another article, my mind racing with uneasy suspicions regarding Eve and her possible criminal activity. I managed to pull myself together enough to write a decent article on green space in the city then bought myself a coffee and a sandwich from a food truck down the street.

As I ate, I questioned myself about how to discover Eve's intentions. I needed to find more to question her about, and I wondered how we would regain the stolen necklace. What else had she taken?

I thought about the mystery Eve had created, a calculating woman at best. On my way home that night, I drove first to Beacon Hill to check out the address she'd given me. It was accurate, an old and elegant building, divided into condominiums. That night I called the Phoenix police and pretended to be trying to find my way to an address, the one given to me by Eve as her mother's. I was informed that the address was valid, and they even gave me directions to the house. At least I'd have that when Eve was gone; I'd still have access to her. I was beginning to suspect everything surrounding this conniving woman. And then I

close to you

wondered what I could do about the necklace? That would be a sentimental piece Finn would more than likely choose to keep. This was getting complicated.

I so wished that I could navigate Bill Sieller's logical mind for suggestions on how to proceed. Keeping this information between Molly and me was an emotional struggle. I was becoming more focused on making life normal again for Granger Finnegan. To be completely honest with myself if no one else, I knew deep within that this man had a hold on me. He was the respectable, intelligent, humorous sort that I had hoped to spend my life with. I found myself turning to a folder containing the few photos I had of him from the first report of his crash and disappearance. His kind eyes had a twinkle to them.

During a break the next day, with a hot coffee in my hands, I walked toward a window overlooking the city. I dialed my parents' phone number just to check in.

"Mom," I began, "thought I'd see how you and Dad are doing. Did you receive the postcard from the Vineyard?"

"Yes, and you have your father all enthused about a trip there soon, maybe in the summer."

I wanted to suggest before then to avoid the tourist season, but I said nothing of that.

"We've thought about it from time to time; we used to love it there when you girls were young. I think your father would live out there happily, but I'm a city gal –

I like it for a weekend, but then I want home. Are you still working on a newspaper project regarding the island?"

I hesitated but then said, "Yes, it's kind of an ongoing issue, and being there is a joy actually."

My mother was quiet for a few minutes, and I knew that my opinion was not hers. As a Boston girl, she had grown up with the world at her fingertips – stores, museums, theater, public transportation – and I knew she'd never want to be too far from Lisa and her family. Maybe it was the first-born thing, the attachment the two of them had for one another. Lisa's life had seemed so well formed – Mom could count on her eldest daughter for consistency, unlike me, who was all over the place.

"Did you call for a reason?" she asked.

I felt shocked. Was she in a hurry to get rid of me? And then before I could respond she continued, "Not that it isn't lovely to hear from you, but is everything all right?"

I smiled and was glad she couldn't see me. "Everything's fine. Just thought I'd check in. I'm painting my bedroom yellow, very cheerful, and my living room tan. Between that and work, I've been keeping busy. I actually need to get back to work, but say hi to Dad for me."

"I will, Dear. You have a nice rest of the day."

When the call ended, I took one last glance outside

close to you

at a sky speckled with clouds and filtered sun. I tossed the now empty cup in a trash can and walked back to my desk. The approaching weekend would find me on the island, intently looking for a sign of Granger Finnegan and our dog.

*****

In the middle of finishing painting the last wall in my bedroom, the phone rang. It was Molly. She cleared her voice a couple of times before speaking.

"Must tell you," she began, "I'd bet my tulips that Finn was in the area today."

"Why do you think that?" I asked as I washed the paint brush at the kitchen sink.

"I was in the yard poking around, watching for my lilac trees to bloom, checking on the lavender and basil for signs of life, when I saw a car with a man and a dog, a dog like Prancer, go past the house very slowly. It was as though he was checking to see if all was well. A few moments later, the same man, same dog, same vehicle, drove the other way. They must have turned around to have a second look. I'm telling you, Cara, I feel certain it was Finn."

"Did he see you?" I asked as I sat down at my kitchen table.

"I don't know. I was roaming around by tall shrubs; he might not have caught a glimpse of me. I'm not sure he would have reacted if he had, this trip inland might have been a closely guarded secret."

Of course, I thought, he would have wanted to keep his very existence unknown.

"That's true," I began, "Finn may know nothing of Eve's whereabouts or Tony's demise. The sign for renting the house is still there. Has anyone stopped to inquire about the rental that you know of?"

"Not a soul. I think it was Eve's way of going along with that fiendish boyfriend of hers. Those two deserved one another."

I thought about what Molly had said, that they deserved one another, which made me think of Jillian. Perhaps moving to Arizona, near to her grandmother, would be a better arrangement for the quiet little girl.

"I suppose there's no way to get that emerald necklace back without outright accusations that she stole it."

"No. I've thought about that a lot. Without alerting her to the idea that we suspect she's been up to mischief, we have no choice but to let it go for the time being. Besides, she told me it was a gift. How could we prove otherwise?"

"Makes me wonder what else she took. The Finnegan family had money, all self-made. They were hard workers. As a new bride moving into this house, Anne Finnegan was about fifteen years my senior. She was very kind to me, helped me plan my gardens, gave me her friendship. They had one child, George, Finn's father. I discovered after I came to know Anne that they'd had another child, a beautiful little girl named Charlotte. She was killed on the sidewalk right in front of my house by a drunk driver. She was only four."

"That's terrible. It must have been hard for her to stay there after losing a child."

"You know what? Anne told me it gave her comfort; she felt little Charlotte's spirit there. Once my son was born, Anne was very helpful – they had a son, I had a son. I soaked up every bit of help I could grasp. They were wonderful people."

"It must have been hard on everyone when Finn's mother died."

"It was devastating to Finn's father. He adored Cynthia. Losing her was the last thing any of us would have thought possible. And with Finn being just nine, it was a swift decision for the two of them to leave Martha's Vineyard and move back here to Wellesley. I loved watching that child grow into a man, a fine man. When are you venturing out to the island again?"

"This coming Friday. I'll leave straight from work. Any interest in going along with me? I could swing by and pick you up."

"You tempt me, but I'll wait. I think you can do better detective work without hanging around with me in clear sight. If we were to run into Finn, it would be difficult for him to deny knowing me and could make him feel ill at ease."

Chapter Eleven

When Friday approached, I went to work with a small bag packed for the weekend. Leaving Boston at four, I arrived at the ferry at six and bought my round-trip ticket. Every time I stood on the docks and thought of the prospect of seeing Finn and Prancer, I had an assortment of chills run through my body. I picked my own brain as to what I was thinking. Was I trying to determine Granger Finnegan's welfare or was I saturating myself in what I was feeling for man and dog. I knew, but I wouldn't even say the words aloud to myself.

At the motel room, I checked the time – just before eight. I knew The Watermark Café was open until ten, but I was starved. I didn't take my coat off, just left my overnight bag and went back to the car.

I pulled into the café's parking area near to the front door, turned off the engine, and opened my car door just as Granger Finnegan pulled in beside me. I didn't know whether to get back in my car, to stand there like a statue, or to go into the restaurant for my dinner. I looked away from him as quickly as possible and then walked with haste in my steps to the door. As I would have closed it, the door was held by a large hand with narrow fingers. I moved as rapidly as I could toward the hostess and my small table. I did not look up until I'd ordered my wine and food, and even then, I barely glanced his way. I watched as he studied the menu, glasses half hung against his well-shaped nose. When he closed the menu and removed his glasses, I looked away but felt his eyes on me.

Each bite of food I managed to direct toward my mouth almost choked me as I tried to maintain my composure. Why couldn't I just introduce myself, say thank you for the warm gloves, how's Prancer? I was making absolutely no sense to myself. At least, I thought, he was still on the island.

I lingered over my dinner so that I wouldn't have to walk past where he sat when I finished. I ordered a coffee to prolong my stay, then watched as he paid his bill, bought an island newspaper, and left.

Within moments, I walked toward the door, saw that his car was gone, and headed outside. The wind had kicked up, and I gathered my hair together so that it wouldn't sweep over my eyes. Slipping into the car, I sat there for a moment and thought about how individual my life was, how there was no one with whom to share my day at work, the story I was working on, my hopes, my dreams. I was grateful for finding Molly, yet I needed more than a good friend; I wanted a partner through my sometimes jumbled life. I wondered if Granger Finnegan wished for that, too.

That evening I read from a book I'd been hoping to read and made myself a strong cup of tea. The instant coffee in my room was not up to par; I would have preferred the real thing. With TV on low and my book in front of me, I fell asleep somewhere around ten and at two in the morning made my way to bed.

Saturday morning I woke and felt joy at knowing that Finn was still on the island and that there was a chance I would once again see Prancer. I took a quick shower, dried my hair, then slipped into jeans and a sweater. With my jacket zipped against the wind, I walked to the office where I found an assortment of muffins and freshly brewed coffee. I chose a chocolate chip muffin and sat down with it as Jim walked into the room.

"Nice to see you, Cara. How are things going for you?"

I gave Jim a smile and indicated that everything was going at a good pace. I told him I'd painted my bedroom and living room and that I was going to hunt for two reddish-colored pillows for my sofa.

He sat down across from me and talked about his grandchildren – it was a cordial conversation. It felt relaxing to listen to generalities rather than speak about particular editorial pieces I'd been asked to write and then the ominous situation regarding Eve and her criminal strategies. I'd begun to feel depleted, yet found the island's offerings to be a renewed sort of life.

When I left the motel for a walk, I headed away from The Narrows. I needed a break. The land I chose to explore was less ragged with rock formations and wisps of sea grass on tethered dunes. I stopped after an hour of picking my way over clumps of seaweed, having found a few pretty stones and shells and two pieces of green glass. I dusted the sand from them and placed them in my pockets to admire closely later.

I thought about Granger Finnegan; seeing him at the café was coincidental, yet he lived nearby. I hoped that when I walked the other way, toward his home, I would have a glimpse of Prancer. I missed him more than I'd missed almost anyone else, comparing losing him to a cat I'd loved at my grandparents' home. Someday, I thought, I'll have a slew of animals running around my feet.

With no particularly good place to sit, I turned to walk back toward the motel, a good hour's journey. Once there, I looked toward The Narrows, saw no sign of life except for a few seagulls, then decided to head into Edgartown to search for my red pillows. In a shop there, I found exactly what I wanted. I liked symmetrical designs and found fire engine red pillows with a white scallop shell motif. They would be perfect on the dark brown sofa back in Prides Crossing. I bought myself a cup of coffee and two tangerines, which I consumed on my way back to the motel. There I read from my book and relaxed after walking and a successful shopping trip. So far this trip to the island had been well worth the time and money. Knowing that Finn was still there was the significant part of the weekend. Now just to see Prancer.

That evening I was tempted to go to The Watermark Café again for clams but decided to drive on to Menemsha for clam cakes instead. Once there, at dusk, I found a small table in a tearoom and settled where I could watch passers-by as they strolled the quaint village. I was about to leave when Granger Finnegan walked into the place and ordered quahogs and a sourdough roll with butter. He chose coffee for a beverage then took a seat at a small table six feet away from where I sat.

I turned my head toward the street, away from his eyes, took a few swallows of my water, then quietly, carefully, stood and made my way to the door. What, I wondered, would I say to him if ever he spoke to me? He knew my name. I wondered if he knew I'd covered his crash more than a year ago – that I was a reporter. Would he have taken note of the reporter's name, me? Of course he'd be watching to see what the world of Boston had decided when the plane was sure to be found. Sending Prancer to him was a dead giveaway – he had to conclude that I was on his side, that I suspected the truth.

close to you

I wondered briefly why he hadn't called Molly again. He'd apparently sent her the poinsettia plant at Christmas, yet he hadn't actually spoken with her. Was he, perhaps, concerned that at her age of nearly eighty he didn't want to involve her in his entanglement? From all I'd heard of him, he was the type of person who wouldn't burden anyone with his unsettling circumstances. Of course, the message he'd left had been about Prancer, and Finn now had him. Maybe the dog was all he'd really cared about.

Once back in my room, I changed into pajamas and settled down with my book. I read for a few hours without a break, then close to midnight, slipped into bed. I lay there for several minutes reviewing my day. It had been good, every bit of it, and I was grateful. Then I wondered if there would come a time when I would actually be brave enough when face to face with Granger to tell him I was glad he was alive.

I pondered my absence of dreams. With so much centered on this case and the story behind it, I was dismayed at why I had not dreamed of even a particle of it. Maybe I was already experiencing overload, or maybe I was so entrenched in daily doses of Granger Finnegan and Prancer that it was all my system could take. A few times I had to talk myself into meditation, or at least trying to, so that I could rest my mind.

Sunday morning brought the sound of church bells peeling and sunshine squeezing in between the venetian blinds in my room. I stretched and thought about what I would do that day before catching the ferry back to Woods Hole. A quick decision had me deciding to skip the motel's offering of a muffin and coffee and to drive back to Menemsha for hot tea and pancakes. The place I favored served their breakfasts with slices of orange and a few grapes on the side. I hadn't been there in years, but I'd noticed it was still a thriving little business when I'd been in the village the day before. It was time to explore other offerings. Menemsha was a dearly favored memory of childhood; I would make sure to bring my parents when they came to the island.

For the remainder of the day I walked around the area close to the motel, keeping my eyes busy watching for a glimpse of Prancer. As I turned to go back inside my room, collect my belongings, and head for the ferry, I saw my beautiful dog. He was doing as his name implied, prancing around as he welcomed circling seagulls ten or twelve feet above his head. I smiled at the happy scene then noticed Granger further back toward the house staring my way. Adrenalin flowed into my chest and abdomen as I turned away and continued toward my room.

During the ferry ride and then driving back from the Cape to Prides Crossing all I could think of was that Granger and Prancer were still on the island and seemingly happy. I was so relieved that this devoted pair had been reunited.

While sitting at my *Journal* desk on Monday morning, I pondered a story I'd been asked to write when there was nothing of significance I had to tackle. In the middle of making notes the phone rang and I found myself talking to Rob at the police station.

"Cara, on your visit to see Eve in the hospital, did she by any chance give you a permanent address?"

I shifted the phone from my left to the right. "I have a Beacon Hill address where she was staying for a few days, then her mother's in Phoenix. Why, has something come up?"

"The hospital called us; apparently Eve dropped a necklace and they had no address to contact her. I picked it up and plan to return it to her."

"I have the feeling, Rob, that the necklace may have been a family heirloom of Dr. Finnegan."

"Well, without him to file a report, I can't do much. But I'll take that under advisement when I go to deliver it. If I think something suspicious is going on, I'll create some other reason for being there."

I gave Rob the two addresses Eve had given me and asked him to let me know the results – I promised nothing would go beyond my own ears until he gave me permission.

With the phone in both my hands, as if it was heavy enough to need extra support, I felt shaky. What had Granger Finnegan been living with for months? This woman was deceiving. I found myself confused with thoughts regarding this case. Over and over I delved into a new article to compose and finalize when along came the Finnegan case. I considered leveling with Bill, but every time I had that urge, I thought about the fact that he would want to know everything, that I could be putting the doctor in danger. I simply could not make that decision.

I sat back in my chair and thought about the found necklace. Had Finn really given it to her? I hated that this woman was Jillian's mother – how was that child going to grow up with any direction in her life? Maybe the grandmother was the answer – I hoped.

I wrote up the article Bill needed for my Wednesday column then walked to the coffee room. Standing at the window, I watched as birds circled a building to my right then flew off to a flat roof where they settled. Once there, I saw that they were pigeons and I smiled. Most people in the city were quick to shoo them away, but I liked them. Their slow movements and trust that someone would offer them crumbs from a sandwich made me realize that I rarely asked anyone for assistance.

That evening at home I put a flatbread pizza in the oven then sat on the sofa and admired my red pillows. I wasn't big on souvenirs, but the pillows were both needed and a warm reminder of a place I loved. As the timer went off for my pizza the telephone rang – Dad often said everything happens at once.

The caller ID indicated that it was Rob McCloud's personal line, not the police station.

"Hi, Rob. What's up?"

"I'll tell you, Cara, this case gets more and more perplexing. I stopped at the Boston address and was met by a guy who assured me that while he knew Eve, she wasn't staying with him. As he spoke, a little girl appeared in the background, long brown hair, big blue eyes, cute little thing."

"That sounds like Jillian, Eve's daughter."

"Yeah, I was thinking that. He shooed her away and then tried to give me a brush-off. This guy had money, Cara, his place was posh; his clothes were top-notch in style. I went back to the station and dug up what I could on him. His name is known in business, but no one can figure out how he makes his money because the business is pretty much nothing. I think it's a front for something dubious."

I thought for a moment and wondered how Eve had made this person's acquaintance. Could she have been tangled in his so-called business affairs?

"So you didn't return the necklace then?"

"No, I wasn't leaving it with him."

"I have to wonder if Tony was involved in this man's business – I'm suspicious."

"You and me both," Rob said with a deep sigh. "I need to question Eve. I'm going back there tomorrow and wait it out. If he tells me she's not there again, I'll sit nearby and wait. She's skipping off to Arizona soon, at least that's her story, but I want to talk to her directly. In the meantime, I'm going through some mugshot books – there's something too familiar about that guy."

"Does your captain know about this?"-

"Yeah; he told me to find out what I could. Frankly, we'll be glad to see the end of Eve. We've already notified Phoenix that they have a one-woman circus coming based on the company she kept."

"Wow, I can't believe Doctor Finnegan was subject to this kind of unrest. In attempting to do a good deed, he may have actually endangered his own life."

"Poor guy," Rob said, "and if that's the case, he paid the price with his life."

At that point I swallowed and thought how deceitful I was being to both Bill Sieller and now Rob McCloud. As far as they knew, Granger Finnegan was gone.

"If you hear anything else, could you let me know, Rob? I know this is police business, but I promise you, it will go no further than me. I do think there's more to this situation."

"I hear you, Cara, and I think so, too. I'll give you a call when I hear more – I'm not dropping this ball."

I held the phone for a moment then remembered the pizza. It was a bit crispier than I'd planned, but still tasty.

Chapter Twelve

By noon the next day I'd finished an interview with a business owner and his immediate staff. Having just moved into the Boston area, they had jobs to offer, yet issues with the ongoing parking in the city remained unresolved. I would have liked to offer my two cents worth, but I was there to report, not to advise.

Back at *The Journal*, I went to the café on the first level and bought soup and tea. I took it back to my desk, punched in some information from the morning's business, then called Molly.

"I don't think we've heard the end of Eve," I said. "Can't really discuss it other than to say she's hiding more than we thought. Anyway, how are you doing?"

"I'm good. The sniffles are long gone, and I'm ready for another nice visit from you. When are you coming out this way?"

I smiled. "Well, there's nothing regarding my work in your direction, but I could pick up some food and bring it with me for dinner some evening soon."

"Phooey on bringing outside food – I can still cook. What would you think of homemade minestrone soup?"

"That sounds delicious. I'll bring an apple pie – there's a shop near here that has great bakery items. What do you think?"

"Apple pie sounds delightful. When can you come?"

"Tomorrow would work for me, maybe around six. How does that sound?"

"Perfect. I'll make the soup today and let it rest. It's always better when you give the veggies time to become acquainted."

I laughed at the idea, but I understood what she meant. "Okay then, I'll be ringing your doorbell around six."

The remainder of that day was filled with writing and polishing the article from the morning's interview. I stared at the computer, finding that I needed to read and reread what I had written – I was distracted by thoughts of Eve, then of Granger Finnegan and Prancer. I was definitely divided in thought. I needed an evening with Molly.

*****

As I pulled into her driveway the next evening, I turned the car's engine off and sat for a few moments looking at the Finnegan home. It seemed desolate and that made me sad. I wondered if the doctor and his dog would ever live there again, near to Molly, back to a form of normal. I felt my eyes become moist and wiped them dry. From all I'd heard from Molly, this family had been close to one another, had loved living in this graceful old house. Yet due to an act of kindness from the young doctor, the place was now abandoned.

Slowly, with the pie in hand, I opened the car door and walked to Molly's front step. As I was about to ring the bell, she opened the door with a big smile and reached for the apple pie.

"Do you smell that soup? It's a good batch, I promise."

I hung my coat in the hallway and agreed, the soup aroma wafted through the house with temptation.

Walking to the kitchen, where we always ate, I admired Molly's furnishings and again, her taste. The décor was plentiful yet not overdone.

"Come and sit down," she urged. "Now would you like a glass of wine or would you prefer to start with hot tea?"

I immediately thought of the peony cups I so admired. "I'll have tea, thank you."

Molly insisted on being the server; I was to be the comforted guest.

As she sat down with the teapot in her hands, pouring two cups full of the steaming brew, she asked about Eve. "What's that devil up to?"

I smiled at the apt label as Molly stared at my eyes. *The windows to your soul*, my grandmother had always declared. I covered my lap with a white linen napkin then looked back at Molly as she passed me the warm rolls. "Eve may be involved in more than we thought. I can't divulge too much, it's with the police. But she definitely has some curious ways in which she operates. My main concern is her little girl."

"Does the child seem alright?"

"I haven't seen her that much, but when I did, it seemed that Eve was protective of Jillian. I keep hoping that motherhood is her strong point – I'm not so sure about her ethics."

"Well then, let's hope the police figure out what she's up to."

I nodded as I accepted the butter dish. "I just hope that there isn't a reason to lock her up. I don't know what would happen to Jillian; although, there's the grandmother in Phoenix. Eve told me Jillian was out in Phoenix, but it sounds from my contact at the police station as if she's still in Boston. I don't know, Molly. Sometimes I think I'm too tangled up in this entire affair."

Molly took a bite of her roll then looked at me as she dabbed her mouth with a napkin. "Well, yes, you've become entwined just as I did, because we both care about a wonderful, innocent man. Have you seen any more of Finn and Prancer?"

"Yes, I saw them both the last time I was on the island. From a distance. It's perplexing – I wish I had a way to get information to him without scaring him to death. I feel certain that the man I see is your Finn, but he most likely has no idea that Tony is dead. He may also not be aware that Eve and Jillian have vacated his home. Obviously he's been off the island, probably with a rented car, at least if that man you saw was really him. But Tony's accident, if it was an accident, wouldn't have been a news item."

"That's true. And did you notice that the For Rent sign is gone?"

I swallowed a sip of tea and looked toward the Finnegan home, barely visible in the early evening. "Where's the sign? Who took it down? I didn't even notice it was gone."

"I have no idea. It was there, and then it wasn't. I suppose it could have been Eve, but my thoughts are that it was Finn himself. I'm sure he didn't take kindly the idea of some stranger renting his house. The Finnegans loved that place – that family stuck together and loved one another."

I took a few ladles of Molly's delicious soup and thought about all that had been lost through an act of good will. It couldn't have been Granger Finnegan's choice to abandon his medical practice years before reaching the age of retirement.

"You know," Molly continued, "I could see you and Finn together."

I nearly choked swallowing soup then patted my mouth dry.

"You'd be perfect together, and besides, you'd be reunited with your dog."

I sat back in my chair and smiled at this woman who had become a confidant and dear friend. "I haven't even spoken to your Finn," I said softly, "and maybe never will."

"Now why would you say that? If Finn comes back here to live, at least during the week, you'd see him when you visit me. We aren't disbanding once this is over, are we? No, that won't happen. So at some point, the two of you are going to collide."

I laughed. The word *collide* had a comical air to it mingled with this subject.

"I can't understand how the two of you haven't met at the island. You gave him a wonderful offering in parting with Prancer. Why couldn't you two speak? You could inquire about that fuzzy creature?"

"Our paths have crossed a number of times – we seem to frequent the same restaurants, but neither of us has ever spoken to the other. I mean, what would I say to him? He must wonder why I'm there, so close to where he lives, and that was a complete coincidence. He gave me gloves at Christmas, signed with a paw print. I may be worrying him with my presence. He might think I'm observing him for a story – that I might reveal his whereabouts."

Molly nodded. "Yes, that's true, but if you spoke to him, you could let him know that Eve is leaving,

close to you

Tony's dead, and that you're not a threat."

I shook my head as I reached again for tea. "It's not that easy. Things with Eve are still a mystery – it could be messy trying to deal with this until she's either jailed or gone."

We were companionably quiet as we finished our meal, deciding to wait for pie. I changed the subject by asking Molly where she had acquired her peony collection – the colors and elegance of the flowers fascinated me.

"Everything was accrued in small, often unexpected finds. My husband was aware that I loved them and brought me several items, and I found quite a few pieces myself. My eyes found peonies almost everywhere I went. They're so lovely but short lived in nature."

"Do you have live peonies as well?"

"Oh yes, you must come when they're in full bloom – I truly think they're more beautiful than roses, although the roses last longer. Finn gave me two of my peony plants, one in pale pink, the other in white. He is such a dear boy, Cara; he deserves someone like you."

I looked away, enjoying seeing a built-in hutch containing varieties of crystal stemware. I imagined that in her younger days, Molly might have been very social, enjoying cooking and inviting guests to dinner.

"Do you think he'd move back and resume his practice?" I asked.

"Definitely. This is a man who loved his vocation as well as his home. I could see him loving the island for a getaway, but Finn would never withdraw from medicine."

After pie and coffee, I collected my coat and thanked Molly for a wonderful evening. It was after ten when I reached Prides Crossing and I wondered why I was there. I liked the name of the town: it sounded like something from a Bronte novel, and I liked living near the water. Other than that, admittedly, I was lonely. Sometimes I owned up to the fact that my choices were not always based on logic.

*****

Toward the end of the week I wondered if I wanted to head to Martha's Vineyard again. I knew that I did, yet I wondered if it was just too much money being spent to get there weekend after weekend – the drive to Woods Hole, the ferry trip, and the motel expense were not cheap. I thought about summer easing its way in and thought how it would probably not be feasible to go up against the tourists. The idea of not seeing the island, and Prancer, for the entire summer was unappealing. I belonged there; I could feel it in my bones. With that thought in mind, I decided that it was soon to be early May and I might as well enjoy the island as much as I could before June when rates were sure to skyrocket. I used the computer to order my round trip tickets.

close to you

*****

As I stood on the ferry's deck, the wind tossing my hair over one shoulder, I marveled at the glimmering sunset against the green-blue waves tipped with white caps endlessly in motion. They echoed in my soul, *Never give up, never give up*. I was excited about this trip, couldn't wait to be there, and felt positive that I'd made the right choice.

Stepping onto land, I looked around at the flow of people, as early as it was in the season, already finding magic in the island. The very notion that it was separate from the rigorous tactics of daily life drew the stressed to a place where they could renew their spirit and find time to meander, to relax amidst nature.

I walked to Jim's car rental and was given the same car I'd had before. I wondered if this was a plan on Jim's part to keep me feeling acquainted with the island, familiar, as though I belonged. It worked. He'd even left my room key in the car for me this time. Having the same vehicle, the same room at the motel, it had begun to feel like home. It crossed my mind on the drive toward The Narrows that I wouldn't mind spending my life here – maybe work on a small newspaper like the island's *Schooner Gazette*. Or maybe Bill would let me work from home – just commute in a couple of days a week.

I pulled into my regular space at the motel and saw that a light was on in my room. I took a deep breath in thanks for the kind people seeing me through a complicated time. Surely Mary and Jim must have wondered what brought me here so frequently, yet they didn't inquire.

I took my overnight bag into the room, where it was warm as well as welcoming, a muffin waiting – chocolate chip. I could feel my lips spreading into a slight smile just as my heart was filled with gratefulness for these kind people. I looked through my living room window toward The Narrows and saw sprinkles of light coming from the house where I pictured Prancer at the feet of his friend, perhaps with a nice wood fire glowing.

It was close to eight when I headed out to The Watermark Café. People there, the hostess and the waitresses, were getting to know me. They probably assumed I lived on the island, and since I was always alone, that I preferred my privacy; no one ever asked me questions beyond what I would like for dinner.

As I sat in that room overlooking the dunes, I watched the door for a familiar face. I did not see anyone I recognized and admitted my silent disappointment. As unnerving as it was to encounter Granger Finnegan, I wanted to.

There it was, an admitted thought: I wanted to see him; in fact, I longed to see him. That evening I dined without a glimpse of anyone other than the serving staff and a few strangers. My meal finished, I felt the urge to

close to you

get out of there, to get back to my room and the warmth of pajamas and a book. Before I could finish a chapter, I was asleep, the sound of the waves lulling me into serenity.

Sun across my eyes alerted me to morning and I turned onto my side, then onto my stomach. I tried to find a little more rest, but the mind is stubborn and willed me to get up.

It was just six-thirty when I pulled on a thick gray sweater and jeans then walked to the office lobby where the usual assortment of muffins and coffee waited. I'd broken the chocolate chip muffin in half, eating that portion as I combed my hair. I would skip another muffin but would gladly have a cup of good coffee.

"You're up with the gulls this morning," Jim greeted me with a smile. "Did you have a good rest?"

"I always have a good rest here – the ocean, as powerful and fierce as it can be, has a way of delivering a sense of calm. Do you ever get used to it?"

Jim grinned. "Lived here all my life. Nope, never get tired of seeing or hearing the crash of waves. This island has everything for Mary and me. There are enough shops and restaurants to satisfy our needs, and no matter where we go, it's wild and pretty. Every once in a while Mary likes to go to the mainland to visit our other daughter, and once a year we head to New Hampshire. Mary's sister lives there, and we enjoy the visit with relatives as well as the mountains. Other than that, we're content."

"That sounds wonderful – a little diversion to the North Country and then back home to the island."

Jim nodded then took a swallow of coffee.

I sipped mine, allowing the steam to escape as I watched the ocean from the office window. "I like the way you've planned this room. You have windows to the parking lot and windows to the sea. That was clever – your design?"

"Actually, it was Mary's idea. Since we need someone in the office, whoever is on duty should be able to see the ocean, to enjoy the morning sun and the evening sunset. We love it here."

I smiled and realized that I felt completely relaxed. Being at *The Journal*, I was always on alert to a new assignment. Often my current assignment would need to be put aside to work on something more urgent. When I was at Prides Crossing, I was alone, away from the city and family. I wondered about my personal planning system – maybe I was getting tired of living solo; maybe I would start to accept a date here and there. People asked me out, just not the *right* people.

As if reading my mind, Jim asked, "Do you have a fella? Seems to me a pretty young thing like you should have someone special in the picture."

I cocked my head to one side. "There have been a couple, disappointing in ways I couldn't handle. I suppose I'm fussy."

Jim nodded. "You should always be fussy about having a partner. I knew from the first time I saw her that Mary was it for me. She took her time, but, luckily, finally felt the same about me. So, no one in the picture just now?"

I shook my head. "I've been working for over a year on a particular story. It's taken my energy to a different level – I really haven't had time to think of dating."

After a bit more small talk, I walked to my car and wondered if I really wanted to go off. Part of me wanted to walk toward The Narrows to see if Prancer would come bounding toward me again. I longed to kiss his head and ruffle the fur at his neck.

I started the engine, switched on some music, then drove toward Gay Head and the cliffs' brilliant color. I walked for nearly an hour when I decided I would drive to Menemsha again for clam cakes and tea. It was liberating to realize that I could go where I wished, eat what I craved, and no one was going to tell me to do otherwise. Maybe that was why I wasn't so anxious to have a permanent partner.

I thought of my college years when I'd tried my hand at poetry – I liked it, the professor liked it, and I thought maybe I'd try it again. This place was rich in sensual details of pertinent displays, nature at its best. I stopped in at a small shop and bought a four by six notebook and a new pen. Maybe I would write something symbolic of the island's charm, or maybe I would write about Prancer, the immediate love I found in him, the heart-wrenching pull when I surrendered him to unite man and dog.

Much had been learned in those days at school when I was being primed for the journalist I'd thought to be. It came as a surprise to me when *The Commonwealth Journal* hired me before I'd even graduated. I discovered later that a professor had recommended me as being detail oriented and with a "flair for word appreciation." I wasn't sure what all that meant, but I was thrilled to be less than twenty-two and employed by a nationally recognized newspaper with honorable records.

Inside a café, I munched on two clam cakes and a cup of hot tea. I watched the passers-by and thought how there were more people roaming the village than there had been the last time I was here. I frowned internally at the prospect of being overrun by the vacationers who were sure to fill this space with so much activity that I would need to relinquish my territorial hold on favorite settings. Was I being selfish in my thoughts? Yes, I was, and I supposed that hundreds of others were thinking similar thoughts, their lives altered by the two-week, one month, all summer visitors who were looking for solace in the sea just as I was. I reminded myself that I must share.

Outside, with a deep breath of salt air in my lungs, I

close to you

walked to a pier where several small, colorful boats were moored, looking ready for a summer sail. I smiled at two seagulls who perched on the bow of a blue boat, each of them looking around as though waiting for their captain to arrive and offer a voyage. The usually strong scent of fish was missing – too early in the day, I thought, the fishing crews weren't back yet.

I turned from the docks to the village and marveled at the quaintness of it all, the simplicity. No electronics stores, no shoe shops, no unnecessary gadget stores – just comfortable cafés, practical offerings of swimsuits and sunglasses, and here and there, a bookstore, a souvenir shop. It was charming and in no way demanding.

When I left Menemsha it was close to three – I'd had my exercise at Gay Head and my sustenance with delicious clam cakes. I was ready to head back to the motel where I could sit outside my room in a rocking chair and simply listen to the sea and its creatures while the sun added a layer of color to my face. I made myself a cup of tea and took it outside, looked toward The Narrows, then saw what I had hoped for, Prancer and his friend walking slowly on the slice of sand before the rocks. They didn't notice me, and I was glad – those few moments afforded me the opportunity to observe them and be glad that they were together.

I sat down in the rocker where I couldn't see them yet felt fulfilled, glad for their happiness and glad for being so near to each of them. There was something satisfying and magical about sharing the same space, the same air, the same love for the area. I shut my eyes to the sun and let its warmth spread over me.

Within minutes I opened my closed eyes as I felt something rub against my right leg – I looked to see Prancer at my side, his excitement visible, his beautiful body quivering with recognition and what I determined was joy. I quickly looked to see if he had come unaccompanied and it seemed he had. I rubbed his ears, kissed him, then told him over and over how much I missed and loved him. This was the gift I treasured. I found each greeting an offering, each parting a heartbreak. He lay down at my sandaled feet then stood up, as though he felt divided.

"I love you, Prancer, but you can go. I know you're happy."

The dog looked at me with his beautiful brown eyes, wagged his handsome tail, then turned and looked toward The Narrows.

"Go," I whispered, and when he obeyed, I murmured to myself, "Come back to visit me again, Prancer. Please come back again and again."

When dusk was near, I thought about going to The Watermark then reconsidered. I drove to the local market, bought fruit, a cupcake with strawberry icing, and a good cup of coffee. I returned to my room and stayed put for the evening.

Almost as soon as the sun made itself known Sunday morning, I packed my items together and left.

The ferry gave me time to think, to analyze my intentions. I watched the waves and the horizon, finally clear with my thoughts – I wanted to find a way to inform Granger Finnegan of the accident involving Eve and Tony. And I needed to figure out a way to tell him about the emerald necklace he might want back, and yet, I didn't want to appear to be a scheming woman trying to get his attention. I was certain that with his good looks, his compassion and intelligence, many women would do summersaults to gain his awareness. Not me. I could respect him from afar – I wanted a man who would see my value, as meager as it might be, and think I deserved what attributes I returned to him. Then I realized, this is why I'm unattached – this is why I'm standing on the ferry's deck alone: I contemplate too much.

Chapter Thirteen

Arriving home that evening, I left my overnight bag and purse in a chair as I walked to the phone; a blinking red light let me know there was a message. Caller ID indicated the call had come from Rob McCloud. With pangs in my stomach for what I might hear from him regarding Eve, I listened. He simply asked that I return his call on his private phone when I had a chance.

I grabbed a bottle of cold water from the kitchen and then sat down next to one of my red pillows from the island. I punched in Rob's number and waited less than two seconds for him to pick up.

"Cara, glad to hear from you. There's nothing urgent, but interesting. And again, this has to be off the record – this is just between you and me."

"Of course," I said as I swallowed a few sips of water.

"This Eve is a tricky woman. I went back to the Beacon Hill address you'd given me to clarify a couple of things that didn't have a finishing touch. She was there, this time with her daughter at her side. She's leaving for Phoenix tomorrow, which is both good and

close to you

bad. I think she could be helpful in a drug case we're on – turns out that guy she's living with is a top-notch criminal with a long list of aliases – we've been after him for years, but had no address until now. He was affiliated with Tony – Tony was a drug runner; this guy imports the stuff through Florida."

"Wow."

"We've been aware of his activities but never had an accurate location for him or knew what name he was operating under until now. Who would think a felon like him would be on Beacon Hill? He makes a lot of money, lives in a posh setting, but that's not what was ever known before. We have a sting operation set up for this guy; it may take some time to rake him in. The thing that troubles me is that Eve had that necklace; if she took that, there's no telling what else she may have that doesn't belong to her. She's leaving, and we have no grounds to stop her or search her bags. That's going to be a problem; we might never see her or whatever she stole again."

I took a deep breath and wondered what I could do without jeopardizing the drug situation. It was all happening too fast.

"Rob, all I can say is that I have her Phoenix address, the same one I gave to you. How did she seem?"

"She tried to be cool as a cucumber, phony. I feel sorry for her little girl. She seems quiet, not like a happy kid. I have a daughter her age; she's like a jumping bean. You know what I mean?"

"Yes, I thought the same, but having been a child with medical issues, I suppose that makes a difference."

"Yeah, you're right. Well, I just wanted you to know that Eve and who knows what else she took, are leaving the area. But in the meanwhile, we now have an advantage over this drug czar – with an address to watch, we'll wrap him up tight.

"Have you learned anything more about Dr. Finnegan?"

I froze. I needed an answer, so simply said, "Well, we all believe he's lost, but without a body, none of us really knows, do we?"

That seemed to satisfy him. When our call ended, I sat with the phone in my hands and felt appalled at the mistrust we needed to develop regarding strangers – I thought that was a shame, and then I thought about how much easier it was to love a dog.

After changing my clothes, I called Molly. I told her I'd seen both Finn and Prancer, that Prancer came to see me, and that they seemed well and content. Then I told her about Eve leaving for Arizona.

"That woman has been nothing but trouble," Molly said. "Except for helping that child, Finn really let his guard down with Eve. He'll probably never see whatever she may have taken again."

"I know – I've thought that myself."

close to you

We were both quiet for several seconds, then I dared to ask, "Do you think he cared for her?"

"For Eve? Goodness sake, no. He couldn't have. She wasn't his type at all. I was shocked when she moved in and relieved when you told me they hadn't been married. None of it made sense until then.

"I'll be happy to tell you, Cara, Finn was fussy. I have no doubt he longed for a wonderful companion, but not a quick, slick woman like her. He had an x-ray technician he was going with for a while; she seemed nice, pretty girl. He discovered she was dating another fellow at the same time she was falling all over Finn. I think she was after his prestige, and maybe his money. I caught on to her, but I kept my mouth shut. Finn figured it out and became *too busy* to see her. He's bright, Cara, in more ways than in the operating room. No, Eve was with him for the child – I'm so glad you discovered what she is, a thief among other things."

"What should I do, Molly? I was actually wondering if you'd want to give him a call. You're old friends; you could tell him about Tony's demise and Eve's leaving."

Molly was silent as I left her time to think about what to do. When she spoke it was with soft, slow wording. "While I think he needs to know what's happened here, I wonder how his accusations, providing he decided to accuse her of thievery, would affect everything else. There's your editor, Bill, and there's Jill. It's complicated, Cara. I do think he needs to know that Tony is out of the picture – I feel pretty certain that man was a threat. I've thought long and hard about the crash. I had mourned Finn's life being taken, then when the investigation proved futile I wondered if there was a possibility that he'd escaped the plane before it hit the water. I can't tell you properly how much gratitude I feel for you having located him and reuniting him with his sweet pet. If I never saw Finn again, I'd be sorry, but I'd be glad that he was safe. I think you should tell him what you can – I could mess it up."

I held my breath and then closed my eyes. She was right; in her anxious and loving way she could reveal more than she should. This would need to be related with extreme caution, especially with the police now watching the drug dealer in question. I felt as though my whole world was like a kaleidoscope of mixed emotions – I had loyalties to Bill that had been concealed – I had Rob who needed my confidence and yet I couldn't tell him what I knew, and I had Granger Finnegan wrapped around my heart and soul for what he endured and for being the type of person this world needed. I felt stumped.

"Cara," Molly began, "am I disappointing you? I feel like I threw the responsibility of telling Finn in your lap. I don't mean to; it's just that I really believe you could relay the information in a more intelligible manner."

"I know what you mean. He needs to know that he could come out of hiding if it was Tony who caused Granger to let go of the plane he loved. Like you, I'm afraid I'll mess things up – I'm going to have to think about this, Molly."

We were miles apart but together on protecting Granger Finnegan. After our call, I sat for a while thinking about Bill Sieller. Would I ever be capable of explaining this to him? Capable or not, I knew that at some point, I would need to be forthright, and I understood that I could lose my job in the process.

Frustrated, I decided a hot bath would be appropriate – time to be soothed and think through this conflict, to remain silent or reveal and to whom.

With the work week before me, I had several days to think about whether I would go to the Vineyard again that coming weekend. I had assignments that would take me out of the office at least two days, then writing them up would further deepen my commitment to the newspaper before personal business. Would I dare to confront Granger Finnegan with the information I had? If it had not been for the drug dealer in Beacon Hill, I could have proceeded without the fear of giving him a head start and evading the police sting. I'd investigated and written enough on the subject to know that dealers had no conscience as lives were destroyed – money was all that mattered. I wanted, as much as Rob McCloud did, to see this monster put away for a long time.

After an interview and back at my desk to begin writing, I sipped hot coffee and decided that I'd better think things through thoroughly before heading out to the island again. Maybe this was the weekend I became a more attentive daughter and sister – maybe. The thought of not being in close proximity to Granger and Prancer did not make me happy. I wondered why I felt the need to punish myself, and then the answer came up and tapped me on the shoulder – I was guilt-ridden with my veil of secrecy.

I expected full disclosure to Granger yet the timing was not suitable – there was too much at stake regarding police business; I owed it to Rob to be diligent with the information he'd generously shared with me.

To keep myself from making the wrong decision toward the end of the week, I called my parents to see what their weekend was going to include. They welcomed me there for dinner on Sunday, or for the weekend, a movie on Saturday, a chance to unwind - I accepted. As soon as our plans were confirmed and the call ended, I felt a pang of longing for the place where I yearned to be.

Arriving at my parents' home in Jamaica Plain, I smiled as I approached the driveway and front walk. Three cats sat bathing themselves on the steps – surely my father continued to feed these visitors as he had throughout the years.

I tapped at the front door then opened it and walked in. The floors, as always, were gleaming and the aroma of chocolate wafted from the kitchen. My mother met me in the hallway drying her hands on a dishtowel.

"So good to see you, Dear," she said with a tight hug. "You're looking a little thin; have you been eating?"

I laughed. "Yes, not your sort of fare, but I eat. I saw Dad's furry friends out front; looks like they've been eating, too."

My mother grimaced. "You know your father. Every scrap, which he makes certain we have, goes out to those little beggars. One of them belongs to Mrs. King, the other two are street cats I think. Your father would have them in if I gave my approval."

I smiled as my father came toward me with his arms outstretched. Then he whispered in my ear as she walked to the kitchen, "They were in all this winter, and last winter, too, down cellar. She doesn't go down there: hates the spiders."

I stifled a laugh and could picture my father sneaking food down to the cats in the warm basement. My mother did not like having animals in the house, which probably influenced my love for having them with me just about anywhere. Like my father, I found them good company.

Asked the usual array of questions concerning

work, boyfriends, life in general, we talked and ate our way through the weekend. When Sunday afternoon came, I drove back to Prides Crossing and wondered what I'd missed on the island – I was getting addicted to the place.

Sitting with a freshly brewed cup of coffee I checked through my mail, mostly advertisements, then checked my phone for messages – all was quiet. I reached for one of my red pillows and stroked the front, thinking about the small shop where I'd purchased them. There were many objects with sea images I thought I might splurge on at some point – maybe a soft throw or a glass bowl to display my collection of sea glass and shells.

The approaching week was heavy with scheduled interviews between the art museum and a new electronics firm. Visiting these places and writing their stories would make my week whirl past, so I knew there'd be little time to plan the weekend five days away. I wondered with a child's state of mind if they had missed me this weekend: Jim, Mary, Prancer, Finn. Of course they didn't, I assured myself – probably never gave me a thought. And I'd enjoyed every minute of being my parents' younger daughter, glad that I'd taken the initiative to be there, allowing myself to be coddled, free of responsibility other than being pliable.

After a warm shower I grabbed an apple from the kitchen and sat on the sofa with a note pad to watch

TV. I wrote a few questions to ask at the electronics firm; their product design had some green energy issues that the public had concerns with. It would be an early night – I was tired; the two days away had been explicitly free of stress, yet different from what I was accustomed to doing. I would welcome the soft bed, the warm quilt, and wished I had Prancer by my side. Then I wondered if Prancer was allowed to sleep with Finn. I wondered, too, more about Finn, and I questioned myself about when and why I was now thinking of him as Finn rather than Granger Finnegan.

That night, I slept and woke as the skies were lighting the day. I'd had a dream involving Finn and Prancer – they were with me. I wasn't sure where we were, but it was an open space where we walked and walked without a single word.

I dressed and felt shaken by the close, if not real, proximity to the doctor and his dog. I found myself thinking about both of them often, not exclusively in dreams. In fact, I realized this was the first time my mind had let me dream of them. Maybe the time apart and distraction of family had been just what I needed.

Walking into work that day, I ran into Bill, and we chatted amiably about our weekends. When we parted ways inside, I felt torn – if a man's life was not in jeopardy, this story surrounding the beloved doctor and the treachery enclosing his existence, I could have been completely candid with him regarding this complicated story.

I sat at my desk, staring at the design floating around on my computer screen, half dazed with the concern I felt for my clandestine way of living the last few months. Forcing my thoughts to return to work, I began the research for my interviews and felt the tension in my body begin to soften and relax. I smiled at the thought of having one of my friend's potent margaritas with lots of salt on the rim. Not much of a drinker, except for an occasional glass of wine when dining out, I was known to get a little light-headed with a good margarita or two.

The art museum story fit perfectly into my personal need for healing as it dealt with Van Gogh, a favorite artist of mine. He'd struggled his entire life, and yet he had dear friends and a talent that drew the world to his side. What troubled him so? Could today's medical methods have helped him to find happiness? I'd wondered about him since high school when my parents had taken me to one of his exhibits. So much of life was about opportunity and fate. I remembered thinking that I wished I could have been his friend, that I could have sat by his side, watched him paint, and told him how much he was respected in the world of art. Yet, would that have been enough? Was a personal life or love the missing equation? I forced myself back to now, to the art museum and its wondrous collection from the world's finest artists.

close to you

Forcing my thoughts back to the museum rather than one artist's life, I concentrated on points I wanted to cover. A new artist was being revealed, a woman originally from Australia now living in France. Her work was said to be revolutionary, laced with brilliant shades of reds and blues no matter the subject. I couldn't wait to see her creations – Europe had been phenomenally impressed. This Boston exhibit would be the first in the United States, giving our museum a reason to boast.

The week went slower than I'd hoped, my mind often drifting to what waited on the island in just a few days. In anticipation of going, I called and made reservations for the ferry, my room, and a car. Then I called Molly.

"How are you," I asked.

"Perfect," she exclaimed. "I have my flowers popping up all over the place, and I just made gingerbread. Want some?"

I laughed. "I'd love some, but this is a killer week at work. Maybe we could plan for a night next week, Tuesday or Wednesday?"

"Of course. Let's do Tuesday; that's closer. Are you heading to the Vineyard this coming weekend?'

Feeling a rush of adrenalin swoop through my body I replied, "Yes, I made the plans and I'll leave Friday night. It's going to get tougher for me since the tourists are already starting to show up on the ferry – I hate to think I'll miss weekends there."

"And do you expect to speak with Finn?"

"Not yet. There's too much going on around Eve. I presume she's gone off to Arizona, though I haven't heard that for sure, but that was the plan. I was told a few things in confidence – I can't discuss them, but it also inhibits me from saying much to Finn."

Molly sighed. "Well, when the time is right, I'm sure you'll handle the situation with grace. What did you do with the past weekend?"

"Visited my parents, which took me back about ten years; I stayed in my old room, which they haven't touched. My room was pink, and my sister's was lavender. I lay there Sunday morning looking at the wallpaper, remembered my mother and me choosing the floral print. It was a bit surreal but nice. My dad had his cats hanging around, same as always. Not much had changed."

"Your father likes cats. How about your mother?"

I laughed. "She likes them outside. Dad always wanted to adopt a cat or two – Mom never approved. He finds a way to feed them; he told me that he even snuck a few in the basement over the winter without telling my mother. It's actually pretty funny – they're very opposite on this, but somehow it works."

"So, you're heading to the Vineyard but you won't see Finn?"

"Well, I quite often see him outside with Prancer,

and once in a while at the restaurant where I go for dinner. But no, this won't be the time I confront him with what I know."

"You're protective of him, Cara. I appreciate that as his friend, and I'm thinking there may be more depth to this guardianship than you portray. Are you sure you're not feeling more for him than a reporter might?"

I half gasped at the question, my mouth dry with the unforeseen query. "I suppose I've been a bit more concerned for his safety than any other I've written about. But his is an unusual circumstance."

We were both silent.

"Are you in love with him?"

I felt like someone had punched me in the chest. Was I in love with him? And, if so, what sense did that make?

"I don't know," I replied in a low tone. "I don't even know if that's possible, or reasonable, to love someone you have yet to meet."

"It happens all the time today, those computer match-ups. When you fall in love without meeting, it's like falling in love blind. You fall for the true person, not how they look."

But I knew how he looked; I'd seen his photos, brushed near to him at The Watermark Café, and yet, I knew what Molly meant. I'd scarcely had a moment to properly observe his face. The photos from before his crash were simple, enlarged of him from a group picture. I'd liked his face from the very beginning; there were signs of character, a person content with himself. Yes, I had been drawn in from the start, and yes, I could be in love. The thought terrified me.

"I guess we could continue this discussion when you come for dinner Tuesday night," she said to my silence.

"Tuesday night sounds wonderful. What can I bring?"

"Just you. Having you come to dinner gives me a chance to cook – I'll think of something, and I'll freeze some of this gingerbread; we can have that with lemon sauce for dessert."

It felt good to laugh, to ease the tension of talking about loving Finn, which I apparently did. "Gingerbread with lemon sauce sounds delicious, and tea of course."

"And tea, of course. Have a great time on the island, and if you get to see that old dog, give his ears a ruffling for me. I do hope to see him and his master back here at some point."

When our call ended, I sat with my hands covering my face. What in the holy world had happened to me that I now understood how deep my feelings were for Finn? How had I not seen this coming?

Chapter Fourteen

The ferry to Martha's Vineyard moved steadily through a choppy sea, white caps demanding notice, the wind encouraging salty spray onto the open deck along with pelting rain. I moved inside, bought a cup of coffee, then sat where I could continue to watch the turbulent ocean.

Once there, my feet on the ground, I felt settled, as though this place was more important to me than where I grew up and where I now used for my own address. No secret any longer, Molly had forced my brain into understanding: what I felt for Granger Finnegan was quite like what I felt for Prancer; I was in love – dedicated to their comfort, to their protection – I had every reason to feel the pull on my heartstrings.

Settled in what I now thought of as *my room* by eight o'clock, I decided on having fried clam strips and coleslaw for dinner at The Watermark. The place seemed crowded when I arrived, but soon after I was seated, it began to thin out; I found myself at one of three tables still waiting for dinner. When I looked to my left, I felt a distinct pounding in my chest as I found less than four feet away Granger Finnegan was sipping a glass of beer. His eyes met mine. The slightest trace of a smile on his nice lips caused me to feel faint, and yet I did not turn away from his gaze. I renewed the thoughts I'd had of him from more than a year ago when his plane and he went missing. He was not classically handsome, yet his features were distinct, saturated in character, every pore appealing.

When I finally had the energy to look away, I traced the dunes outside and then took a sip of my water. Did he know who I was? Did he know that I was Cara Wells from *The Commonwealth Journal*, to whom he gave a pair of beautiful gloves? I so wanted to ask him how he was, and how about Prancer? I wanted to tell him everything I knew, but there was this drug issue I needed to conceal from everyone around me except Rob.

I ate my dinner, as he did, as though I was dining with a plague victim – I made certain not to look his way again, yet I felt his eyes on me. This was awkward. While I wanted to sit near to him and tell him everything I knew, I could not, not now. Trapped in a net of concealment, I felt like a traitor to both Bill and Finn.

Leaving half of my meal on the plate, I left my table, paid my bill, then walked as quickly as possible to my car. I started the engine and promised myself to drive carefully but fast – I did not want any form of

close to you

communication with the dear doctor at this point.

I thought about taking a ride, spring had arrived in full bloom and it was just getting dark. Feeling drained, I opted for my room and TV, and maybe a cup of something hot, instant coffee or tea. Tea, that night – it would be tea.

The next morning, still feeling shaky with having been in close proximity to Finn, I walked to the room where Jim and Mary served their coffee and muffins. With his same jovial smile and words, Jim chatted amiably about it being good to see me, then asked if I wanted some of yesterday's muffins to toss to the seagulls.

"I've seen you tossing them bread," he said. "Thought you might like to give them these seven muffins left over from yesterday – they'll be thrilled with a tasty treat."

"I'd love to. Do you feed them your leftovers when I'm not here?"

"Oh, yes. Why waste food that they would enjoy? Most days we toss them rolls or muffins; they're always grateful.

"Say," Jim began, "do you know the chap with the dog? You know, the one I told you fixes the broken wings and legs on the gulls? I saw him here earlier this morning. He seemed to take an interest in your room, had the dog with him, hesitated, but just kept walking past. I think when I first met him he said his name was

Geoff."

With a shaky voice I said, "You did say his name was Geoff. I don't really know him, but I've seen him a few times at The Watermark; we haven't spoken."

Jim nodded. "Seems to be a nice fellow. People around here like him. Sure does have a nice house there on The Narrows. Mary and I have admired that place for years."

"Who lived there before he bought it, do you know?"

"Honestly, I haven't seen anyone there in years before this fellow. It was once occupied by a summer family then it went empty. Before that, a family lived there year round, but something happened to the mother and they left the island."

I had chills and hoped it wasn't noticeable. Finn's mother had grown ill when he was just nine, which was when he and his father had returned to Wellesley. It all blended in: the trauma of losing his mother, the move to his grandparents' home in Wellesley, and now back to the house where he was born and where his mother died. I wondered if Finn's father had ever sold the house or had just abandoned it as a summer rental for tourists. Jim had told me that the house had been bought with cash, but that could have been rumor.

"It seems they'd had an ideal life here – it's all very sad. I agree with you, it's a lovely old place," I said.

Without want for further conversation, I wished him

close to you

a pleasant day and headed outside.

Having tossed the muffins to the gulls, watching them circle and dip for their treats, I took a deep breath of salt air and looked toward The Narrows. There was no sign of Granger Finnegan and Prancer, but Jim had seen them earlier. Perhaps they'd gone for a longer walk, or maybe they'd returned and were now inside the house. For no good reason, I would have loved seeing them, just a glimpse would have been gratifying.

Without further thought of what I wished, I drove to Oak Bluffs where another ferry was docked, allowing passengers to disembark as others waited to depart. I wondered why on a bright spring Saturday anyone would leave this place that was so energized with endless forms of nature and beauty.

In a quaint bookstore I purchased three novels then took them to a small coffee shop where I browsed what I'd bought. I looked outside to the tourists and maybe a few townies. It was interesting to guess which ones were the tourists. Most often those carrying backpacks and bags for their new-found treasures had ventured out to the island as I had. I smiled watching two dogs greet one another, one a Yorkshire Terrier, the other a German Shepherd. They looked like they might want to play, to thoroughly check one another out, but the Yorkie's mom pulled anxiously on the leash to move along. Dogs were so much easier than humans.

Having walked the town's center, I thought about

what drew me here. Other than the island's rich environment, Finn and Prancer held my interest. I drove back to the motel, left my jacket in the room, and wandered outdoors. I started to walk toward The Narrows when I hesitated, deciding to go off in another direction more inland than edged by the sea. I followed a path laden with tiny shells and stones, each side bordered with wild flowers I wasn't familiar with. Purple, pink, yellow, white, all shapes and sizes. I thought one, the pink, might be phlox. Each bloom was swaying in the wind, as if dancing to music only they could hear. The temptation was strong to pluck a few for my room, but that would not be fair. They were having a great time in the outdoors, alive.

Every thought seemed to take me back to Finn. How close did he come to dying in that crash? He either had to plan to abort the flight just before it went into the sea, or he had to have tried taking it down safely, crashed into the water, and managed to survive. I hoped he'd tell me about it one day – I'd never been able to convince myself that he'd died. Something about the look on his face in all the press photos told me this man had the determined stamina to save his own life as well as those who went under his scalpel. From everything others had said concerning Dr. Granger Finnegan's capability as a surgeon, as well as comments from friends such as Derek Halstrom, this was a prince among men. He was what I had dreamed of, hoped for, in someone dear to me.

I walked for more than an hour with no idea where I was, except on this wonderful path. At almost four I reversed my walk and headed back toward the motel. All I could think of was the fact that I wanted to be near the sea and my room. I smiled thinking of Finn. "Close to you," I whispered to the wind. "That's where I want to be: close to you."

Arriving at my door I reached into a pocket for my key and inserted it into the lock. When my hand went to the doorknob, I found a small piece of folded paper. The note read, *Even though the weather is warmer, I still make good chowder.*

My heart felt as though it came to a screeching halt. No one but Finn could have left this message, an invitation. He'd extended this before, after my decision to leave Prancer with him. I stood feeling powerless to take a step into my room and slowly I turned and looked toward The Narrows.

I saw no one, not even a gull, then after catching my breath, I opened the door and walked in where I could collapse across my bed. There was no way I could accept his enticing offer – keeping the truth from him would be the depth of my own darkness. I could not face him without complete honesty.

Sunday morning brought bright sun and the weight of Finn's note. Surely, he must realize who I am. That I am the reporter for *The Journal*, that I sent his dog back to him and broke my own heart. Now what was I going to do?

Two ideas reached out to me. One, that I would see Molly for dinner on Tuesday evening, which was always pleasant, and the second was to avoid seeing Finn, to answering questions, to conceal what was known, about Eve. Never in my six years at the newspaper did I feel such a massive responsibility toward anyone or anything I'd written about. I felt very small inside a large issue. I swung my legs to the left, bare feet on the carpet as I walked to the front window. No sign of people, just gulls. As much as I didn't want to leave, I decided to pack up my belongings, pull on some clothes, and head to the ferry. I could grab coffee before boarding – I needed to go.

So much of me wanted to stay right there forever, but I could not jeopardize the ongoing police work and I could not risk Finn's life. While it was thought to be Tony who caused the suspected threat, what if it wasn't? What if it was this person in Beacon Hill? What if he had ordered the doctor's demise? It was more than I had expected to find in what first seemed to be an unfortunate, straightforward accident. For the time being, I needed to lay low – an invitation for chowder with Finn and Prancer would have typically been a dream come true, but not yet.

A few hours later I was dropping my overnight bag on the sofa between the red pillows and standing like a

close to you

statue as I stared at the tan walls. This was not the life I'd projected for myself. The newspaper was fulfilling, I loved doing interviews and writing accompanying articles to make it all visible to *The Journal* readers. The rest of my life was personally obscure, until the disappearance of Doctor Granger Finnegan. This man's life had impacted my own – through this investigation I had found Molly and Prancer, two of the bright spots in my somber existence.

I slipped out of my shoes, unfastened my slacks and blouse, then walked to the bathroom to enjoy shower water cascading over my body. I stood there, eyes closed, wishing I was in the sea, feeling the salt spray against my skin, wondering if Finn liked swimming in the ocean, or anywhere. I'd always been what my family called "the fish" due to the fact that I spent so long swimming that I came out of water, any body of water, looking like a prune. I loved the concept of every molecule in me being embraced, my face toward the sky, my heart at its happiest. Soon, I promised myself, I'll find a place to go into the island's water. The area near to the motel was too rocky, but a sandy beach was within a short walk; I would go there, and I would swim.

I thought about calling Molly, but I was seeing her Tuesday night for dinner. I thought about calling my parents but remembered they were occupied with a garden club sale all weekend. Dry from my shower and in a lightweight robe, I sat down on the sofa and thought about Monday's assignment, another set of interviews, several hours of writing to properly express what I hoped to learn. I sighed thinking how fortunate I was to have a position that made me think, anything to divert my attention to something less benign rather than the tension surrounding Finn and Eve's associates. What was the parent of a child doing getting mixed up with felons? I would never understand Eve and her collection of blunders. Attractive, young, well-spoken, why would she involve herself with the likes of Tony? Why would she allow him to become the father of her child?

My mind began to wander. I dialed Rob McCloud's private number and, when he answered, I apologized for calling him on a Sunday.

"Rob, I've had the most bizarre thought. What if Eve wasn't with Tony? What if she lied about him being the father of her little girl?"

"Why would she do that?" Rob asked.

"What if the man living in Beacon Hill, the one you're watching, was actually Jillian's father? Eve would never tell who he was – he may have provided for her trip to Arizona. I think he could have been anxious to get rid of her, keeping her as far away from his illicit position as a drug czar. It struck me funny when you told me that he answered the door to his home and Jillian was there at his side. I could be wrong,

Rob, but it feels right. Do you know what I mean? It makes sense. These people are unscrupulous; they have no shame in being responsible for lives taken through drugs – all they care about is the almighty dollar. Doesn't it strike you as strange that Eve was living there before she left for Phoenix? That address in Beacon Hill was far above her means. What was she doing there? And you said the child was at his side – perhaps she was more familiar with him than we could have imagined – maybe he was her father."

I waited for Rob's reply. We were both still, thinking of the possibility. It was Rob who broke the silence. "You've given me something to think about. Eve could have been lying about going to her mother's place in Phoenix; the address is real, but still, it might not be her mother's. This is a pretty complex situation – this guy here in Boston may be at the center of everything that's happened."

We were both quiet again until Rob began, "You know, you may have a point. The more I think about it, Tony didn't have the class someone like Eve would go for. The guy in Beacon Hill is suave, sure of himself. You could be right, Cara. You could be right."

"You're continuing to watch him?"

"Definitely; it's within our jurisdiction. We're keeping an eye on the property; it's a cooperative effort for the department. We're not stepping on each other's toes, if you know what I mean."

I sighed. "This is getting complex. I wonder if Eve actually left."

"She did – we checked. She boarded a plane with her daughter when she said she would. Frankly, I'm glad she's gone, but this isn't over."

We spoke about keeping one another informed of anything new then ended the call. When I sat quietly, the phone still clasped in my hands, I wondered how this had developed into a multi-level case. I wasn't prepared to do police work; I wasn't accustomed to being a protector. And the deepest issue for me was the deceit. I had information I couldn't reveal to Rob or to Bill, and now I had other details relating to the case that I needed to keep from Molly.

I made myself a cup of tea and sat looking out through my kitchen window until the tea needed reheating in the microwave. Once it was hot again, I sipped it until I could feel the warmth trickle down to my stomach. I thought about Finn out on the island and wondered if he knew more – Rob and I were trying to figure out a reasonable explanation to the plane crash, yet maybe Finn had additional information.

Monday I kept busy, even at home. I focused on finding additional information on my computer that took more time than I had at work. I found it amazing how complex a city could be with both negative and positive negotiations being dealt with on a daily basis – I was often shocked at information that came my way, everything from embezzlement to murder. I found myself questioning much of what I heard from the most innocent of people, knowing from experience that life could be deceiving.

Revisiting my thoughts on the Vineyard, I decided that I would not go there the coming weekend. I wasn't sure how to handle the invitation for chowder, as much as I longed to go. Hopefully, there would be another time when I could be honest with my knowledge and thoughts. Tuesday evening was near. I would enjoy my time with Molly – she was the logic in my life and the one who shared my concern for Finn.

Would I tell her I'd been invited to his home? I was half afraid that if I did, she would encourage the visit. I didn't want to start lying to Molly, but if I kept the invitation to myself, it would be a concealment rather than an outright lie. I couldn't tell her for now – I had no choice.

Tuesday evening couldn't come fast enough. I longed for the sweet comfort in Molly's home and the delicious meal she prepared, along with the warmed-up gingerbread. We consumed our meal with pleasant chatter about my work and her gardens, then she looked at me and asked if I knew anything more about Finn.

I hesitated then told her I'd seen Finn and Prancer the past weekend – they seemed content and playful. I simply omitted his note, his invitation, and therefore the reason for not revealing more information than needed.

I wondered if there would ever be a time when I could be completely honest with everyone. I began to feel that I was climbing a mountain in thin air, running out of breath and feeling depressed. Nothing had ever prepared me to become deceiving – there had never before been a reason for it.

"You're looking tired," Molly commented over a second cup of tea. "Is all this concerning Finn dragging you down? It must weigh on your nerves."

I shifted in my seat and looked away then back into Molly's eyes. "I suppose I'm a little stressed. I've had a demanding workload and then there's this mystery surrounding Finn and why he's hiding, pretending to be someone other than himself. I don't want to make the wrong move, Molly. Everything I do and say is calculated."

"Even to me, I suspect."

I felt and knew I must look ashamed. "Yes, somewhat; I need to be careful what I say for a while."

"Don't feel badly about that, Cara – your reasons are valid. When there's something positive to tell me about all of this, you will. I'd love knowing he's safe. Until then, you do what you must."

I smiled at Molly and said thank you; I was grateful that she understood my plight.

Driving back to Prides Crossing I felt rejuvenated by being with a good friend who clearly understood the situation. We were on the same team, just in different positions. What I'd meant to express that evening and did not was my sincere appreciation of her friendship, for being a sounding board for my concern and dedication to helping our mutual love. I no sooner had that thought then I realized, I definitely felt love for the man I was trying to help. I questioned my sense and sanity.

The remainder of my week was engulfed in a project requiring a full day of research then two days of interviews. I would start writing the article at home and maybe even have it finished before my Monday deadline. The forecast was calling for blustery rain all weekend. I stopped at the store on my way home, picked up some essentials, and settled in.

A couple of times when I took a break for a sandwich or drink, I sank into a squishy chair near the sofa and stared at my pillows. I loved their brightness and the motifs depicting shells. Their vibrant color should have made me happy, yet I felt miserably empty. I forced myself time and again back to the project which Bill would be pleased to see had advanced. I tried harder than ever to please my boss with speed as well as exceptional writing. Or was I filling my own emotional cup? I decided it didn't matter; I was getting the work done while I accomplished distracting myself from Finn and the island.

By Sunday night I was exhausted both from work and from evading the issue that had become part of me.

I went into *The Journal* on Monday morning feeling physically wilted yet emotionally energized with having written a piece Bill would be proud to publish.

Now I had the week before me, with new material to research. The new assignments, while newsworthy for the city, were not half as interesting as the one I'd completed. Some days were like that I reasoned, excitement or monotony. Something light would provide rest for my brain, and that could have turned out to be a benefit, yet it did not. I found myself with too many cupsful of strong coffee and thoughts drifting to the island and its inhabitants.

Managing to concentrate on tedious reports that entire week, I felt the pull to the Vineyard. It was where I felt most comfortable, near to Finn and Prancer, who had captivated my thoughts and existence for what seemed like eternity.

Chapter Fifteen

When a friend from college called Wednesday evening to invite me out for dinner and a classic film being shown at an old Boston theater, I hesitated. I knew it would be good for me to socialize, to get my mind on something other than work and Martha's Vineyard, yet I couldn't even find the energy to get dressed for that casual affair. I made my apologies to Keith and thanked him for thinking of me, but I also didn't want to mislead him. He'd been a reliable companion through four years of school, but there had never been sparks. I thought about Finn – no sparks there, just a massive bonfire of emotion. All I could concentrate on was being near to him and Prancer, even if I didn't get to see them, just being a stone's throw away from them made my heart skip a beat.

I began to think of the island as my refuge, and I began to think of Finn in a faithful, intimate way. His invitation for chowder would surely be about more than testing his culinary skills – we would talk. I could not share what I knew at this point nor did I want to say anything deceptive.

I hugged my red pillows and felt like dissolving into a good cry, but I didn't. I made another cup of tea and drank it as hot as my mouth would permit, then I grabbed a romantic novel and began to adjust. Things would work out in time, I promised myself.

By Friday morning I was debating what the weekend would entail. It was toward the first of June and tourists heading to the Cape and the islands were bumper to bumper. I wanted to go, there was no doubt, but I also wondered what I would do if I came face to face with Granger Finnegan. What would I say to another invitation? If I messed up this chance to know him, to experience a relationship with him and our dog, why would I deny myself that opportunity? He was beyond everything I could have wished for in a partner – everyone loved him, except the one person who may have tried to end his life. I sighed and felt a lead-heavy sensation in my stomach – I could not risk Finn's existence for my own emotional advantage.

By noon, I was calling Jim and Mary to see if my room was available; it was, and a car would be ready when I departed from the ferry. I felt a pang of joy circulate through my system as well as a raging fear for what or who I might encounter.

I boarded the ferry just before dark, having fought a vast array of traffic carrying people for a similar respite on the island. They seemed joyful, giddy with the prospect of being in a sublime space for a few days. I

close to you

felt their anticipation, yet I also felt the profound dread of doing or saying the wrong thing if I was confronted with Finn face to face. I understood that it could happen – it nearly had a couple of times as we dined just a few feet apart. I thought, too, about the coincidence of Finn and me finding the same cafés and having the same attraction for a popular restaurant. He was a man with a house, a kitchen; he could make a good chowder according to his invitations, and yet, he dined frequently at the Watermark. Was I looking for similarities? Maybe.

When the ferry docked and I was in my car, I sat there for a few minutes wondering what I wanted, if anything, to eat before driving to my room. I started the engine and steered in the direction of Menemsha, bought stuffed quahogs and a large bottle of water, then headed for my room. As always, it was neat and welcoming, a chocolate chip muffin wrapped and waiting for me. This was definitely my second home. I wasn't sure where my first home was – maybe at Molly's.

I slipped out of my work clothes and into gray jersey pajamas before consuming the food, delicious as always. With TV on for company more than news, I sat on the small sofa and looked around the room. It wasn't so different than my own place at Prides Crossing – I could have some fun decorating this space to make it mine. I smiled at my presumptive thoughts – Mary and

Jim might have more to say about my influence on their property. I thought maybe I should have been a designer rather than a reporter – I wouldn't be in this mess. I also might never have known of Granger Finnegan, Prancer, and Molly.

I stood and looked out into the dark toward The Narrows, wondering if I could see a light on in the Finnegan house. I couldn't see a thing and pulled the drapes and blinds over the windows. I sat down with a book, switched off the TV, then read until I slept. I woke up early on Saturday morning, used the bathroom, then walked into the bedroom area and crawled under the covers. I thought I'd just warm up, but I returned to a deep sleep until after ten.

I lay there staring at the ceiling, wondering what I would do on that day, how I would endeavor to avoid Finn, and yet he was exactly who I wanted to be near. I allowed myself the pleasure of imagining what having chowder with him would entail. Would he say he knew exactly who I was from the beginning, that he found me appealing, that he longed for a life with someone just like me? I turned over on my side and chastised myself for the foolish thoughts. He didn't know me, but I knew him. I was pretty sure I'd figured him out, that I knew who he was as a man. I concluded that he had to have been lonely, and I nearly inserted into my fantasy that he wanted to be as close to me as I wanted to be to him.

Deciding to get back to reality, I pulled on jeans and

close to you

a jersey, took a light-weight jacket to combat the island's wind, and headed to Jim and Mary's for my morning brew to go. I skipped the muffin with plans to have an egg on toast, maybe in Edgartown since I hadn't been there in a while.

As I drove, I thought about how to compose my day. With double the traffic on back roads, I took it slow and thought first about where to have breakfast, then what adventure I might choose when I'd consumed something healthy.

Edgartown, being a host town for the ferry, was bustling with humans and a fair number of cute dogs on leashes. I was aware of how the islanders must have felt when the season they depended upon for a living was seized by traffic and pedestrians fighting for space in the narrow streets.

Finding a parking space was a challenge, yet I decided that if I left before having breakfast, I probably wouldn't make it back there until the end of summer – the crowds were only going to increase. I found parking near an outdoor seating area at a well-known café, ordered my food, ate it quickly to make room for someone else, then went back to my car.

From there, I drove inland, away from the water, where there were less people. I came across an alpaca farm, pulled to a stop, and stood by a fence to watch the animals graze with a few sheep. After fifteen or twenty minutes I went back to my car and drove slowly through quaint areas where homes were often surrounded by meadows, patches of woods, and even small ponds. The island had not experienced a growth in technology and fast food establishments were an anomaly. What tourists found charming about Martha's Vineyard and Nantucket was their stability in offering tranquility, peace, and beauty.

At a small farm stand I stopped to look at potted plants and an assortment of jams and jellies. It was too early in the season for vegetables, but their signs indicated that when the warmth arrived, so would their tomatoes, cucumbers, peppers, and basil. I could see myself coming back later in the season. I bought two jars of blueberry-raspberry jam, one for me, one for Molly, and a loaf of banana bread to take back to Prides Crossing. This was my kind of shopping – I avoided the typical grocery stores as much as possible.

As I opened the door to my car, placing my purchases in the back seat my phone rang. I looked at the caller's number and saw that it was Rob. Immediately I felt my chest tighten; the tension from thinking about criminal activity was more than I'd encountered in previous reporting.

"Cara, just thought I'd share some interesting information with you. Can you talk?"

I slid into my car seat and closed the door. "Sure, what's happening?"

"You wouldn't believe the complexities in this Eve-

Tony saga. The guy on Beacon Hill is a fellow who goes by the name of Bart – full name Jason Bartlett. He has a pretend business, dealings in day-trading, making it look like he's got a legitimate lifestyle. He's bigger than we thought in the drug trade – Tony worked for him."

"How are you getting this information?"

"There's this thing called a snitch – you know about their kind."

I sighed. Yes, I did. "He knows this Bart guy?"

"He works for him time to time. He also works for us time to time. Anyway, what he's revealed is that good old Bart had plans to eliminate both Tony and Eve – he'd had the car rigged that he'd sent Eve and Tony off in – brakes were tampered with to fail suddenly. He wanted them both gone."

"Why both of them? What if Jillian had been in the car?"

Our snitch told us that Eve and Bart weren't ever married, but you were right, Tony was a henchman, Bart is Jill's father. He wanted to keep the child but get rid of the mother. He gave her an ultimatum, get out of Boston or suffer the consequences. The guy is ruthless. Apparently Eve didn't want to go but had no choice; she knew of Bart's ability to harm anyone in his way. Cara, we're getting close enough to shut this guy down. It's not going to be long. No one feels loyalty to Bartlett; he treats everyone like dirt, except Eve in the beginning. Eventually even she became tiring, and he had thought to raise Jill himself. When Eve survived the crash that killed Tony, he decided to get her back to Arizona taking Jillian with her."

I closed my eyes and wondered how anyone could be so callous. He was actually plotting to kill the mother of his child along with Tony. When I was quiet with my thoughts Rob added, "The day of the accident, Tony was supposed to be driving, but Eve didn't like his erratic style – she drove, which is what saved her. Had the positions been reversed, it might have been Tony that survived and not Eve."

"Wow, it's unimaginable that these vile people are out there, ready to cause major destruction."

"Well, look at the business he's in. The guy deals with major cartels, drugs coming into ports like Florida's as disguised merchandise. He doesn't care who gets killed, through the delivery systems he's developed or through the use of product. He has no conscience, protects number one and builds his bank account to ludicrous amounts. I'm telling you, Cara, I'm itching to put this guy away."

"And you think that will be soon?"

"Give us another couple of weeks – we're that close to nailing him. This guy has been getting away with these atrocities for a couple of decades. This time, he's been messing with a personal issue, his little girl. The sentimentality of the deal caused him to get careless –

between that and the fact that our snitch literally hates Bartlett, he's going down."

I took a deep breath and glanced toward the farm stand, pure in its offerings, so opposite to those who perfected the art of criminal behavior, who took values and tossed them aside. "I'm anxious to hear that he's out of business, Rob. Not that there aren't others who will probably fill in where he's seated at the moment, but one by one."

"Exactly," Rob said. "We don't have a perfect world, but if we can put one of these freaks away every now and then, it's a positive move."

"Rob, any chance I can get an exclusive when you finally nail this guy?"

"Cara, I wouldn't have it any other way. You'll be my first call when we can disclose everything."

With the call ended, I allowed my head to rest against the back of my seat as questions surged through my mind. What could this man, Bart, have done to Finn? Had he felt threatened by a prominent Boston doctor who had saved Jillian's life?

My world shifted. For no reason I could verify, I felt like I needed to cry, to just sob until I'd dry up and crumble into dust. Never before in my career had I come close to anything so deceitfully dangerous. And never before had I fallen in love, or anything close to it, through my work. Granger Finnegan held my interest even after the case was basically dismissed. I wondered what would have happened, what would I have done with my attachment, had readers of the paper not contacted Bill for answers. Would I have gotten Finn out of my system and gone on to career and dating like a normal person? I didn't know. What I knew was that I was entwined in a life I had come to treasure, and in doing so, had met someone with whom I had developed a prized friendship. I could not imagine my life without the influence of Molly Penniman.

I looked in the mirror on my visor and straightened my hair by pushing and pulling at it with my fingers, then I started the engine and backed out of the space. I drove not knowing or caring where I was going – I was moving, I was alive, and maybe I was part of something that would make this world a better place. I thought about Eve and Jillian in Arizona, glad that they were away from harm. Jillian was young enough not to feel the impact of a father in prison, and hopefully, Eve would find the common sense to keep her child safe and in a loving environment. I recalled the child's eyes, the absence of joy in her expression. It bothered me. Then I realized that Bart's reach might extend beyond the Bay State.

At a small café in a location I wasn't sure of, I stopped and bought myself an iced tea before continuing my random journey. Near a small body of water, I stopped and parked near a few other vehicles – I watched canoes and rowboats being directed close to a

close to you

sandy shore and I longed for it to be a bit warmer so I could swim. I watched as a black and white dog came out of the water shaking his entire body, then he sneezed before rolling in the sand. I laughed at his antics and wondered who was going to vacuum that adorable pooch. If I had Prancer with me, I'd have taken him to enjoy the same playful clowning about.

When I drove on, I checked my time – it was nearly four and I thought to reverse my direction, heading back to my room. I would read for a while, maybe outside, facing the sea, and I would prepare myself to dine at The Watermark Café later. No doubt it would be busier than what I'd been used to, but I didn't care; I was wishing for their delicious scallops and coleslaw, and maybe a glass of Riesling. If I had to wait for a seat, I would.

My thoughts as I drove were of Jillian and Eve, their atrocious situation, to the point that the man who fathered her child was perfectly fine with causing Eve's demise in order to have control of his daughter. And did he have other children as well? Men like him cared little for the trauma they caused to anyone in their path.

I found it troubling how opposite Bartlett was to a man like Finn who performed intricate surgeries and kindness to those in need. How did someone like Bart find his happiness, or did he not? Could power and money be so important? I thought about others I'd interviewed over the years, people with homes in the area, homes in the tropics, another in Europe. Did that make them more content or did it just camouflage a general discomfort for life? What I knew was that my parents had lived in the same modest home for thirty-five years, and my little cottage in Prides Crossing was adequate for my style of living. Certain I'd enjoy a place here on the island for a getaway, I'd also be fine with an occasional stay at a motel, just as I was doing. Money was not going to rule me.

I pulled into my space at Jim and Mary's and walked around the building to the actual entrance facing the sea. I stood for a moment taking in the deep green of the water – it seemed to change according to time and temperature. As I was about to place my key in the lock, I noticed Prancer halfway between the motel and The Narrows. I watched as he chose his steps carefully, heading toward his friend, away from where I stood. Suddenly he stopped, turned to look my way, then came bounding back, racing into my arms. I fell emotionally apart. I needed that dog hug – he represented everything good. I sat down on a rock to be more at his level as I stroked his soft fur and kissed his head. For just a second I allowed my eyes to move to where Finn stood, his hands in trouser pockets, looking our way. I wondered if he ever felt concern that I would reclaim the dear creature at my side. Gently, I encouraged Prancer to go, but not before I gave him another kiss on his face. With a longing in his eyes, he turned toward

close to you

Finn, looked back at me, then proceeded to run back toward The Narrows.

That evening, dressed in a knee-length dress of soft cotton, I sat at the restaurant and watched as each person came through the door. Part of me begged to see Finn, but I didn't. I finished my meal and left, leaving my table for those waiting, then drove toward the motel. It was still light outside, the weather mild. I turned my car toward a beach I knew to be sandy, more appropriate for swimming than where I stayed. Just another couple of weeks and I could be there in that water, walking the shore as I searched for my shells and smooth colored glass. The simple things were the most satisfying – but not exclusively pleasing, as I reminded myself of my red pillows back home. I liked to think of myself as practical, yet there I was, on the island again, digging into my savings for the cost of a room, a ferry ride, and a rented car. Did I think I was kidding myself?

Back in my room I slipped into pajamas and sat on the sofa with my nearly finished book. I thought about what Sunday might bring, where would I go for breakfast and exploring before I needed to head back to Prides Crossing.

I thought, too, of the loneliness I had been feeling for the past several months. Most of my friends were settled, some with children, and here I was, mucking about by myself, thinking about a man I might never meet, and if I did meet him, might not have a chance to know. I wanted that chance; I wanted to sit and talk with him about the size of the weeping willows in Wellesley, the peonies gracing Molly's home, his hopes and dreams other than saving lives on a daily basis. I wanted to know him and for him to know me, and I wanted us to find one another irresistible. I was in love with my imagination, or at least someone who existed that way in time.

With Sunday morning bringing an overcast sky, I decided to try for an early breakfast in Menemsha, one last glance at a place I loved before heading back toward Boston. I looked for signs of Finn and Prancer but saw nothing of them before I packed the car, said goodbye to Jim, and headed out. After Menemsha, I would board a ferry and get back to reality, hopefully beating some of the Cape-departing vehicles. It was getting more contrary to contemplate making the choice to leave, for perhaps longer than another week. I needed to develop a resistance to this place, and yet I knew that was going to be unbearably hopeless.

I arrived back at Prides Crossing close to five, glad to have evaded heavy traffic, but wishing I was still on Martha's Vineyard. I dropped my overnight bag, left the jams and bread on my kitchen counter, then sat down and wrote down everything I could remember about Eve, Bart, and their situation.

Chapter Sixteen

I had, at one time, felt destined to be where I was – working at my first choice in newspapers and living in a quaint cottage on the North Shore – everything in my life had felt balanced. Since being introduced to the world of Granger Finnegan through tragedy and wrongdoing, I found each day contorted, twisted away from the norm I was contentedly accustomed to. It was a lesson in my life: the unexpected could happen and dealing with it might not be a simple matter.

"I saw Finn and Prancer," I explained to Molly on the phone the next night. "Prancer came to greet me, which is always a pleasure. He looks healthy and happy, not the dog I first met when he was with Eve. But I don't know how and when to reveal the information concerning Eve and Tony – Finn could think that nothing has changed. But I need to give it more time, Molly. I need to handle this with discretion and let everything else play out."

"I know how hard this is for you, Cara. Protecting both man and *beast* are obviously important to you, and to me as well. There isn't a day I don't think of Finn. I look next door and want to see him in the yard, tossing the Frisbee to Prancer, sitting in his garden with a glass of wine or a cup of coffee. It's been a lonely year without him; I long for lights in the house instead of darkness. I have a pretty good feeling for what you're going through, and I want you to know it doesn't go unnoticed. All you do is appreciated."

I smiled at Molly referring to Prancer as a beast, then looked around at my newly painted walls. "This matters so much to both of us, Molly. I'm hoping it won't be too long before I'll be able to explain everything, to Finn, to you, and also to Bill. My editor is also my friend, and I've been purposely deceiving him for a long time. Where does one draw the line when a life is at stake?"

We spoke for a few more minutes before hanging up. With the call ended and a dinner date set for later in the week, I decided to get a head start for an article on the seven-mile-long Mystic River. A ribbon of blue running north of the city, with problems and attributes, it was noted for both transportation of goods and scenic cruises.

I'd always thought of the towns surrounding Boston to be charmed by the body of water which was historically necessary, connecting one another, enriching our lives. I hadn't lost my interest in Prides Crossing either. I loved the area and my home was small and cozy, ample for me. Yet the island of

close to you

Martha's Vineyard had something I'd never thought much about prior to the Finnegan report and investigation. It had a stoic serenity that seemed independently audible and visible in the people, in the land, its indigenous plantings encouraged by salt air. It was drawing, magical. I could not comprehend how anyone fortunate enough to live there would ever leave.

No matter what happened with Finn, someday, perhaps far in the future for financial reasons, I would find a way to have a small place on the island, a pause from the necessities of life. With that profound decision made, I continued to read and research the river's growth in importance throughout the years. Its significance to the city was obvious, binding the lengthy shoreline to vibrant pleasures and availability to commerce. We couldn't be more fortunate, and I would include that opinion in my article.

My week disappeared faster than I'd anticipated – articles were written and published, new assignments came to my desk. Thoughts for what was happening with Jason Bartlett frequently entered my mind, making me cognizant of the precarious position I was in – keeping Finn safe while being as forthright as possible with my editor. He had questioned nothing regarding the plane crash, and I had given him no reason to suspect that this case had infiltrated my life to the brim.

*****

I went to dine with Molly, and I was more than ready. In her presence I was free to relax – we could talk about Finn which took me to two prominent thoughts – protecting him and caring for him. Molly was on to me – she recognized the intense need I held to keep negatives from embracing his life any more than they had – he'd suffered a massive interruption in his vocation as a surgeon, and he'd been forced to relinquish meaningful friendships. Grateful that he now had Prancer, I still understood his need to communicate with others such as Derek Halstrom, often his flying companion.

As we dined on delicious lasagna and a crispy salad, I looked at Molly and smiled with my question. "What ever happened to our peanut butter toast suppers? This is a fabulous treat, yet I enjoyed those toast and tea nights as well."

Molly dabbed her lips with a napkin and swallowed some wine. "I like the peanut butter delicacies, but it's also fun to cook once in a while. Besides, I'm trying to add a little meat to your bones."

I laughed. "Everyone tries to feed me. I'm really doing okay. I eat apples and bananas, oranges and grapes – healthy stuff."

Molly grimaced. "Don't you cook?"

"Not much. Never paid much attention to what my mom was doing in the kitchen unless she was making cookies. Maybe someday I'll find a husband who knows his way around the kitchen."

"You could starve to death waiting for that, unless, of course, you and Finn hit it off. He loves to cook – he used to make a stew no one could resist. Tomato based, everything in that pot – so good. He always brought me an ample amount, some to enjoy at that gifting and more to freeze. If he ever gets himself back here, I'm getting that recipe written down. He also made the most creative salads – added watermelon and bleu cheese to a variety of vegetables, then a great raspberry dressing he concocted himself. That man, I'm telling you, is a keeper. I often picture you two together."

I sat back in my chair as I sipped wine and digested what Molly was saying. She had Finn and me together, and while I was silent, my thoughts were in agreement.

"How does one land in the company of Dr. Granger Finnegan?"

Molly's shrewd eyes watched my own. "You just be who you are – he'll find you. He's already invited you for chowder – do you think maybe he's given you a hint that he's interested?"

I leaned forward, placed my wine glass down, and took another bite of lasagna. I looked away for a moment, out to the gardens now visible with summer-evening sun. "It could be that he knows who I am as a reporter – my byline gives that away. But personally, he really doesn't know me."

Molly shook her head. "Wrong. You sacrificed that

dog you loved, the dog you willingly took when he needed a home, and then you gave him up to a joyful reunion."

"But Finn didn't know how much I cared for Prancer – he might have thought I was just doing a good deed."

"Cara, Finn is smarter than that. Why do you think that when he sees you he sends that dog over for a little love?"

With another mouthful of lasagna, I thought about what Molly was saying. I sipped some wine and looked at her. "I'm pretty sure the dog makes that decision."

"Oh," she began, "you're a doubter. Let's just see what happens when you're more at liberty to be open about what's going on. I accept that you can't reveal everything to me, and I understand that this complicated case is not settled enough to talk to Finn about it, but at some point, yes, at some point you're going to be unencumbered by those necessary secrets. I have confidence in you, and I have expectations that you and Finn, and that hairy dog, are going to be a unit."

My heart skipped several beats – I smiled at Molly but could not bring myself to be honest enough to claim that I hoped she was right.

"You know what he did on my seventy-fifth birthday? He made me pancakes and brought them over to me – there were three, all with different smiley faces,

close to you

and he decorated them with fruit pieces to make them look like they had hair. He also gave me a beautiful cupcake he'd bought at a bakery, pink icing with a candle in the center. And later that day, a bouquet arrived. That night he requested the honor of taking me to dinner, my choice where. I requested his house and something simple. He made one of my favorites, beef stroganoff with the most scrumptious mashed potatoes, drowning in butter of course, and we had strawberries with sweet cream for dessert. I'm telling you, Cara, this man is a catch."

I looked at Molly and felt my eyes clouded with moisture. I dabbed at them with a napkin, and while she noticed, Molly said nothing of my raw emotions. "You're very lucky to have known someone so caring."

Molly took a long swallow of her wine. "You're going to have that, too, Cara; I can feel it my bones."

I wasn't so sure, but I'd certainly allowed the thoughts into my daydreams, anticipating a charmed life with man and dog.

"Heading to the island this weekend?"

I shook my head. "No, I'm saving my pennies as well as my soul. I need to gain some perspective on this whole Finn matter. There are bits and pieces to see finished, and that's not yet within my control – I need to be patient, and in the meanwhile, I hope Finn doesn't make a move from where he is and how he's living. This weekend I think I'll plant some flowers around my place and just hang out there."

Molly smiled. "That doesn't sound like a bad idea. I find great comfort in my gardens and then being in this nice old house with a good cup of tea."

I nodded. "I love the sound of that. And I'm actually thinking of shopping for a pet."

Molly laughed. "A dog? A cat?"

I swallowed my last bit of lasagna and said, "No, I'm thinking a rat."

Molly's expression went from a smile to a pair of lips in shock. When I looked into her wise old eyes, I laughed.

"You're jesting, right?"

"Nope," I said, "I like rats, and having one would be good company. I can keep it in a cage while I'm at work, a nice, roomy cage, and when I come home, I can have it out with me in the house. I need some companionship."

"A rat?" Molly's voice had reached an extraordinary pitch with disbelief.

"Yes, a rat."

That Sunday, after planting purple and yellow pansies all around my yard, I went to a local shelter and stood trying to decide on the white one or the gray one. I discovered they were both females accustomed to one another – I adopted them both, along with a small pet carrier and a three-foot collapsible cage. I questioned their food needs and bought that at a pet store along

close to you

with water bottles. I could have had my weekend on the Vineyard for what I spent, but I loved them. Ruthie and Rosie became my roommates – and when they didn't nibble on my new red pillows, I was perfectly delighted with their company.

When I first spoke with Molly on Tuesday evening, I didn't mention the rats. We talked about Finn, we chatted about the gardens we both enjoyed, and finally she asked, "So, you weren't serious about getting a rat were you?"

"Not *a* rat," I answered holding back from laughing. "Two rats, Ruthie and Rosie."

"Cara, you're teasing me."

I laughed. "Just a bit, but I do have these adorable creatures running about in my house. One is gray, the other white."

"I don't care if they're blue and green," she said in horror. "I cannot imagine having a rat for a pet."

I laughed again. "Well, Ruthie is on my lap and Rosie is in the window enjoying sea air through the screen. They're really quite cute, but I promise not to bring them when we next dine together."

"Thank you for that."

I smiled as I stroked Ruthie's sleek body – they were company, and I rationalized that I saved them from somebody's large snake. I did not like raptors and other carnivores who relied on fresh meat.

Molly continued to chat about her gardens and plans

to enlarge a space for additional year-round greenery. "Something like Boxwood or Holly," she said, "a provision for the birds to hide from snow and wind in the winter."

"You're able to do exactly as you choose," I said. "That's what I'll do when I own a home – with a rental, I'm not to plant more than seasonal flowers."

"You'll have a home someday," she said.

When our call ended, I sat thinking about all I would do with my own home. I allowed myself to imagine living next door to Molly – if you're going to dream, dream big.

Proud of myself for staying on the North Shore that entire weekend, I found myself braced for the week ahead. Bill had given me choices of columns to write. With a cup of coffee and a little research, I chose to interview and write about a heart specialist who had made remarkable improvements in surgery and recovery. I arranged an appointment for that Wednesday, and the column would appear in Friday's edition.

Walking into the offices off Massachusetts Avenue, I found myself in what looked like a nice, not extravagant, hotel. The receptionist was cheerful and helpful, the seating was comfortable, and the walls were decorated with a few choice paintings reflecting the work of Edward Hopper, a favorite of mine. I had a good feeling about this place, and when I met the

close to you

doctor, a gentleman in his fifties, at least six feet and three or four inches tall, all I could think of was Abraham Lincoln. He extended his hand to me, and we walked into his office, a room with a large window, a desk, and two chairs.

"As I recall," he began, "you covered the tragic loss of Granger Finnegan."

That acknowledgement sent chills through my body. "Yes, I did."

"He was one in a million," he began. "This city was fortunate to have him; we miss him terribly. Once in a while he and I had dinner then played a round of racket ball; we joked that we could have dessert if we worked it off."

I smiled. "Everyone I've spoken with about Doctor Finnegan has had kind things to say about him."

Our conversation went on to the technicalities of heart health, the new medicines that were working miracles, the procedures made simpler than the old way of slicing into the human body, creating long periods of recovery.

"People of all ages need to know how important it is for our bodies to be a bit spoiled," he said. "Smoking, drinking in excess, too many nice desserts, no activity – those things hurt us. Sometimes we inherit the unfortunate problems we develop, but even then, staying fit helps us to live with our issues. It's so important."

The voice he spoke with was articulate and gentle, as though he cared with every fiber of his being. I found the interview fascinating as well as heart-warming. These wonderful doctors were heroes.

When I had the information from Dr. Sanchez, I shook his lean hand, thanked him, and went back to the office with more material than I had imagined to work with. I wanted to portray his gentleness, the missing arrogance found in many physicians and surgeons. Dr. Sanchez had a sincerity to his words which added to the complicated explanations he offered to the general public.

The entire time I spent writing the column on Dr. Sanchez, I couldn't help but think of Finn. He was out on that island, a man accustomed to the operating room and intricate mending of brain tissue. How he must be missed, I thought. How many patients are going without Dr. Finnegan's expertise with procedures he had developed? It bothered me to think that more than a year had passed without those skilled hands and that brilliant mind restoring lives, creating magic. I wanted to get Finn back to Boston.

With Friday's column concerning Dr. Sanchez making its start on the first page, I was thrilled for the man and for me as a reporter, but I also thought about Finn seeing this article. *The Commonwealth Journal* was available everywhere; certainly he would see this report on his friend and that it was written by me. I was glad about that – I wanted him to understand my dedication to my work, and more importantly, the subject matter. That he knew Dr. Sanchez was another plus – the two of them seemed similar – committed to saving lives without pomp and circumstance. They were men with a grace-filled purpose.

When I went home that night, I left my portfolio and handbag on a chair then went immediately to free my little rodents. They were waiting; both stood on hind legs as if asking about a treat. I fed them then watched as they scurried around my living room. Simple as they were, I found them consoling for my lack of another companion. I thought about taking them to the island when I went again, in their little traveling carrier, but then where would I allow them to be free? If they nibbled on the curtains or even the woodwork, Jim and Mary would not be happy. If I went again soon, I would confine them to their cage with plenty of food and water – surely they could be comfortable for a couple of days at home.

As I ate my soup and salad, I watched their antics and smiled – those two were busy little individuals who made my life better with their chases, their rearranging of my pillows, and their efforts to break into my cupboards. They were like little felons looking for an easy pilferage. Having something to take care of, my father said, was a joy. He was right; Ruthie and Rosie were no trouble and absolute fun to watch.

That weekend was the second one in which I found myself at home. In mid-June the Vineyard was going to be mobbed, and I wasn't sure that I could still have my room. I was finding ways to keep occupied, yet I longed for the island's ability to make me feel complete. The fulfillment came from doing nothing more than being there, or was it being close to Finn? I convinced myself that there was something remarkably mystical concerning our selected locations on the Vineyard – he just a football field length from a room chosen for me. That alone was amazing and enchanting.

Chapter Seventeen

Early Monday morning I cleaned out the girls' cage, fed them, and left for work. I didn't mention the rats to anyone other than Molly, not yet. Maybe I'd break the news about Ruthie and Rosie at some point, but then, why? I had a few close friends at work, but not anyone who needed to know that I adopted two feisty rodents. Everyone thought of me as efficient, and some said I was sweet, but if I brought up the girls, where would that take their opinion of me? My life, my pets, no one needed to know, except my family. At some point I would gently reveal that I had two roommates. Dad liked cats – I wasn't sure about rats. Mom was going to tell me she would not step foot in my house ever again.

With a pending assignment on my desk, I focused on researching three businessmen and college administrators who were trying to make a difference among students struggling to pay their tuition. I liked the idea of people who have money and power trying to aid those who have little or nothing.

After reading about each one of them, I set up appointments to interview them separately, then as a group. I wanted to hear their comments when together – this was important information.

When I'd finished arranging times for the interviews, I sat back at my desk and realized this was going to encompass the entire week. I looked forward to embracing the questions I hoped would result in thorough information about when, where, and how. Each man was interesting, their ages ranging from forty-one to seventy-eight. Each had success written all over them, and obviously, their motives were in line with saints – help those in need.

Before I could begin writing the introductions, the phone rang, and I found Rob at the other end of the line.

"Sorry, Cara, I left your private phone number at home; I hope it's okay for me to call on your work phone."

"I guess it's okay, but if it would make things easier, I could call you back on my own phone. You know, a little more privacy."

"Yeah, good idea."

"Okay, hold on for a few minutes – I'll go get a coffee and talk to you in the hallway."

Rob agreed and I hurried off, anxious to hear what news he might have. I dialed his number and he picked right up. "Anything new?"

"Yeah, we're ready to pounce on Jason Bartlett. He's bigger than we thought in this mess. This guy forces the average guy, like poor Doc Finnegan, to use their small planes to transport some pretty potent stuff. If they don't agree, guess what – he threatens them with harm to their families or harm to the pilot. We have information on him that is going to put him away for a long time, maybe for life. Anyway, in a day or two, there's going to be a confirmation of his activities and a raid on his house – he's done, Cara, in a day or so, he's gone."

I took a deep breath. This could mean that I'd be free to tell everyone the truth. This could free Finn from hiding out on the island. This was about to change everything.

"You there, Cara?"

"Yes," I said. "I'm just trying to grasp the importance of this without falling on the floor. I can't believe this could be coming to an end."

"Yeah, I know. This guy has been responsible for murder after murder – It's just a shame that he probably tried to coerce people like your doctor friend – he had so much to offer the medical world."

I held my breath, another time when I wanted to reveal and explain, but I had to wait. What if the raid on Bartlett's home found no one there? What if this nightmare continued?

I thanked Rob profusely for keeping me informed and asked that he give me a call when the agony of this issue was over. He promised I'd be one of the first to know.

Finishing my coffee, I went back to my desk. I tried to settle my mind on a very interesting piece of reporting, yet found myself wrapped up in seeking the finality of a long and painful list of secrets.

With an unwavering determination to concentrate on the three gentlemen I was to write about, I settled in, and when through with the basic prelude to what was going to be a major article. I sat back and felt confident that this was going to be significant. And if what Rob revealed to me was about to happen, my life was about to become a cut above what it had been in recent months; I couldn't wait.

By the time Wednesday afternoon came around, I was emotionally exhausted. I had hoped to hear from Rob, and yet I was immersed in the feature essay. Proud of this assignment, and grateful that Bill had given it to me, I had one last interview, the one with all three men together. Then the writing would begin in depth – a piece that was going to confirm my importance to *The Journal*.

By Thursday morning, everything was set – the trio interview went perfectly, the writing flowed. Bill was ecstatic. Other stories were set aside for the following week as Bill made this the Sunday feature.

Thursday evening as I fed Ruthie and Rosie the phone rang. Rob's number was clear as I felt the adrenalin rush stomp on my entire body.

"Cara, are you sitting down?"

close to you

I immediately sat down, missing Rosie by about an inch. "Did you get him?"

"Sure did. It was a combination of sources, our department and federal guys. This Jason Bartlett was a wild one; he was involved in drug delivery to this country, to Canada, to Aruba, all over the place. He has more money accrued than we could possibly imagine. It's done, Cara. It's over."

I felt my heart skip a few beats as I closed my eyes and took a deep breath. "Anything on Eve?"

"Eve was roped in like so many others; she was duped into doing some of his dirty work, partially because of her daughter's brain illness. Your friend, the doc, he fixed that, but Eve was still tied to this monster. She's living with her mother and has been being observed in Phoenix. Looks like she's settled in, has a job in an accounting firm. I think we can kiss her goodbye unless she's needed to testify for old Bart's trial. Nothing will save him – he's cooked."

I felt the tension leave my body. No more lies, no more avoiding Finn. Now I wondered how I would explain to people who mattered – I owed Bill, Finn, and even Molly, for the hollow information I'd feigned.

Rob and I set up a time the next morning when we could get together so that I could write up the article, letting Finn and everyone else know that the whole mess had been finished. With our call complete, I rested my head against the back of my sofa and closed my eyes again. I felt one of my girls scamper across my lap and opened my eyes to see Rosie checking out one of my red pillows. I scooped her up, found Ruthie in the kitchen, as if she was thinking of baking a cake, then placed them in their cage for the night. I took a shower, allowing the cascading water to wash away the stress of dealing with danger and truth, or lack of it. I had a new life before me.

With a lightweight jersey pajama bottom and a sleeveless t-shirt on, I rubbed my wet hair with a towel and sat back down in the living room. It was nearly nine o'clock, but I felt so relieved that I decided I needed to tell my parents how sorry I was for not being quite myself in recent months, and maybe for longer. The Finnegan piece had bothered me from the beginning. I'd felt horrified and helpless when a young, clever, and radiant doctor might have been sacrificed.

My conversation began with my mother, anxious that I'd put myself in danger. I assured her that I had been tense, but safe. My father was more inquisitive, wanting details. I could not divulge the particulars, like the names involved, not yet, but I gave him an accurate account of what had transpired. They were stunned, yet told me they were proud of me. I changed the topic and told them about my Sunday feature – they were ecstatic.

I couldn't call Molly after talking with my parents – the conversation drained me. I would tell my dear friend the next day, before I tried to get a room on the island.

That Thursday night I slept as I had not in a long while. The fatigue enveloped me, and I slept soundly, waking early and phoning Jim to see if there was a room for me. Yes, he declared happily, they'd been saving my room until Saturdays when they had the feeling I wouldn't be out that weekend. He welcomed me back and said there'd be a car waiting at Oak Bluffs. I made my reservation for the ferry and felt like a brand new person.

When I arrived at *The Journal* on Friday morning, I walked to Bill's office and told him about Bartlett and my exclusive. He wasn't happy that I'd kept everything from him, but he understood. And the fact that Rob was letting me be the reporter who broke the story, even though it wasn't my usual type of assignment, impressed him. I promised he'd have the piece by the end of the day, then went to meet Rob.

During a break from my writing that afternoon, I called Molly. She didn't answer right away and that frightened me, but when I called later, she explained she'd been out in her garden. I told her our worries were over, but I didn't give her the particulars – she didn't need to know about Jason Bartlett's ill doings, just that all was going to be settled and, at last, Finn could be told.

"Would you like to be the one who tells him everything is okay, that he can come home to his old life?"

"No," she was quick to reply. "You're going to Martha's Vineyard this weekend – it's time to meet him, Cara, to tell him the truth. That dear man needs to know that his hiding days are over. You can do this, Cara, and tell him to come home, tell him we'll set up that little farm stand he spoke of, him selling radishes, me selling violets. And tell him how much I love him and missed him. He needs to come home."

With our call complete, I smoothed the tears from my face, walked to the ladies' room to splash cold water on my eyes, then patted them dry. I went back to my desk and finished my article for Bill, taking a copy for myself and my face-to-face with Dr. Granger Finnegan.

At day's end, I drove to my cottage, left plenty of food and water for the girls, tossed a few items of clothing into my overnight bag, and headed to the ferry in pretty heavy traffic.

The vibration from the engines beneath my feet on board was suddenly noticeable. I watched the waves being cut by the ferry's progressive insistence and marveled at being able to enjoy the voyage. Previous trips had been riddled with tension. Now my heart was anxious but light. I needed to concentrate on Finn and Prancer – there was about to be an important transition in their lives.

I thought about Eve and wondered what Finn would

think of her taking the emerald necklace. It had been his grandmother's, her birthstone, and certainly a family heirloom. I had to think about how to approach him. I didn't think I could show up at his door and ask if the chowder was still an offering. I thought about leveling with Jim and Mary as well – but that would have to be Finn's decision; he'd been known with a different name, a name that reflected his actual initials. He and I had some explaining to do.

When the ferry docked, I felt my heart racing. As much as I wanted this admission of truth all around, I had no idea how accepted it would be. I hadn't been a saint; I'd lied over the years when put in a precarious situation, but nothing had been misleading or harmful – white lies to prevent further dismay. I recalled a work friend asking me how her hair looked when she'd had it cut extremely short. There was no putting the long hair back anytime soon, so I told her the cut was stylish, flattering. What I neglected to tell her was that the flattering style might have been appropriate on someone else, but she definitely looked more appealing with shoulder-length hair. The misleading words I spoke to Bill, to Molly, even to Rob, had been to protect. Surely that couldn't have been harmful.

I paid for my rental car and drove to the motel. Most of the parking spaces were filled; I pulled in close to my room and took a deep breath. When I stepped out of the car and went into the lobby, I found Mary there.

She looked up from a phone call and smiled when she saw me. Waiting until her call was completed, I gave her my credit card as she told me how nice it was to see me.

"I made certain to get chocolate chip muffins in your honor," she said. "We're so happy to see you back here, Cara. We've missed you."

"I'm glad to be here, and thank you for taking such good care of me. You and Jim are so kind."

I wondered later as I dined at The Watermark, still crowded with patrons after nine at night, if Mary and Jim would be as fond of me once the truth was revealed. I had never been deceived to my knowledge, and I wasn't sure I'd like it – certainly they would feel somewhat the same.

Back in my room after dinner, I turned the lights low and sat on the sofa. I thought about what Saturday would bring, perhaps an apprehensive attempt to see Finn. I thought, too, of my little rats, alone for the first time since I'd brought them to my home. Poor little things might wonder where I was – maybe next time I'd bring them along. I smiled in the dim light thinking of them. No one had been thrilled to discover that I'd selected little rodents for company.

Being on the island again felt right – with a responsibility to set the stage for truth, I went over in my mind what I would do first. Taking a deep breath, I realized that everything I'd been living with for months was about to change. My first duty was to Finn, and while I was about to deliver information that was bound to ease his life, I felt like a teen with a first crush, awkward about confronting this man, hopefully without blushing, without shaking. I then thought of Prancer – I would see him as well, and for that I felt pure joy. If nothing else, I hoped that Finn and I could become friends, and that we could share the benefit of Prancer's company.

I sat for a long time playing the meeting out in my mind. His invitations for chowder indicated that he was not annoyed with my presence on the island, and what I had to tell him was certain to ease his concerns. Sometime after midnight, I forced myself to go to bed. Awake with anticipation until after one, I drifted off and was surprised to wake with sunbeams across my bed.

My first thoughts were scattered with tension – I reasoned that I should be jubilant about finally seeing the end of deceit. After a shower and donning a knee-length dress in hues of pink, I brushed my hair and slipped my feet into tan sandals. I was ready for summer's warmth.

Without thinking too much about Finn, I walked to the host room of the motel and found both Mary and Jim there, smiles of welcome on their faces.

"Have we told you how nice it is to see you again, Cara?" Mary began. "We were so afraid you'd had enough of us here on the island and that we might not see you again."

I poured myself a small amount of coffee, enough to feel the caffeine's pull, and then sat down. I took a sip as I looked up at these two dear people. "I've missed my time here; it's a favorite place." I hesitated before continuing. "I hope that when I've explained a few things to you, you'll understand my being here sporadically."

Jim and Mary looked at me as though I'd just announced that I was an alien, expectation for my words waiting on their faces.

"I need to talk to someone, today hopefully, and after that, I'll tell you more. I've loved every moment of my stay here, but there's been an ulterior motive. Nothing terrible for those you know, but…oh, I'm not being clear. Please, trust that I will tell you this weekend what's been happening over the past several months. There's nothing to fear; it's really all about renewal and joy."

They looked at one another then at me. Jim was first to speak. "Cara, we suspected there was something going on. You know, a young woman like you without a relationship in sight, we figured a broken heart might be the culprit. Whatever it is, you owe us nothing, but if you trust us enough to tell us, Mary and I are all ears."

I smiled at them and half whispered thank you. I looked forward to explaining everything before the weekend was over.

When I left the motel, I walked in the opposite direction from The Narrows. I wasn't prepared to walk over to Finn's house, not yet. I wanted more than anything to unburden myself and him of the once lurking criminal intent that had been keeping us in a bubble, stepping carefully through life. I was exhausted with the secretiveness as necessary as it was – my life, and Finn's, would be changing for the better.

After an hour of slow walking, I turned back toward the motel and The Narrows, making the trip in just twenty minutes. I was ready. With my eyes to the sea and standing on the motel's rocky shoreline, I caught a glimpse of Prancer bounding my way and smiled through tears. Seeing him brought me pure happiness. He brushed against my bare knees and I knelt down to stroke his fur and wrap my arms around his neck. After several minutes of an affectionate greeting, I looked up to see Finn watching us. I stood then hesitantly whispered to Prancer, "Wait here for me."

I went into my room, scratched a note on a slip of paper, then went back to Prancer and tucked it around his collar. Once fastened in place, I gave him another kiss on his head and told him he could go. Again, he gave me a soulful look with his dark eyes and then I watched as he leaped over rocks to Finn's side. It took a few moments before the note was detected, but then I watched as Finn read what I had briefly written. He looked up at me and I shivered. Within moments, Prancer was back at my side with a direction written on the other side of my note, *Tonight, seven. Yes to the chowder.*

Chapter Eighteen

At six forty-five Saturday evening I was both exhilarated and unnerved. Having showered and tried on the few garments I had brought with me to the island, I ended up in the only sandals I owned, an ankle length light blue skirt, and a short-sleeved white blouse.

The breeze was gentle, more so than I'd known it to be, and while I felt certain that this evening was going to be an enlightenment for Finn, it was going to be terrifying for me to come face to face with a man I'd known only through the eyes of others – how did I fall in love through this entanglement? Would he live up to the person I had created by piecing what I'd learned about him?

With a last glance in a small oval mirror by the door, I walked outside, looked toward The Narrows then carefully made my way over and around the rocks. I was standing at the front door to a charming house when I heard the muffled bark I was so familiar with, and then the door opened. Finn looked radiant, as if he knew that I was there to deliver good news.

We stood looking at one another, Prancer nuzzling

my right hand, each of us barely moving. It was finally Finn who stepped back and said, "Please, come in."

I stepped inside and marveled at the simplicity of the place, the views of the ocean spectacular through large windows I could not have seen from the motel. Prancer brushed against my skirt as though protecting me – he wasn't going to leave my side.

I turned to face Finn who had stopped to observe my moves. He invited me to sit down and smiled at the dog who was claiming me.

"Can I get you a drink?" he asked softly.

I sat down on a sofa, Prancer at my side. "Yes, that would be great," I said in a voice so low I wondered if he'd heard my reply.

"There's iced tea, sparking water, rum, red and white wines – does any of that sound right?"

"The iced tea would actually be wonderful."

He disappeared into a dining room and then what I thought to be the kitchen. When he returned with two iced teas, he sat across from me in a roomy chair. We looked at one another, me with uncertainty, Finn with confidence. He waited for me to speak, his eyes traveling my face.

"Thank you for inviting me."

He smiled just enough to let me know he heard me. "My pleasure," he said.

It was my turn again – I felt tongue-tied in the spotlight. He stood, walked away, and came back with a

close to you

biscuit for Prancer then sat down again and looked at me. "The chowder is hot; would you care to have some now?"

Before I could answer, he stood and reached across to me with his left hand, which I accepted.

"I think the dining area is a nice space, but I set us up over here by the windows where the view is best. Please," he said as he walked me to a small table where he'd placed two chairs, a table nicely set, a bouquet of wildflowers in the center. I sat down like a robot and he walked away, returning with a tray containing two ample bowls of chowder, two garden salads, and a basket of small bakery rolls and butter. I stared at the food and did all I could not to cry. This was unimaginable even a few days ago.

"Are you alright?" he asked in a low voice.

"Yes, I'm sorry."

Finn spread a white linen napkin across his lap, took a sip of his iced tea then looked at me.

"There's so much I need to tell you," I said as my eyes met his.

"If we have our chowder while it's hot, the three of us can sit out on the deck to watch the sunset. Meanwhile, I'm delighted to have you here – I've been an ardent fan of your columns for years."

"You have?"

Finn nodded and smiled. "Yes, when you made your debut with *The Journal*, I thought, at last, young blood, innovative ideas, fresh expressions."

I took a sip of chowder, which was the best I'd ever tasted then looked up at Finn. "Then you read the initial article I wrote regarding your crash."

"Yes. And it was tactfully composed. Thank you for that."

We finished our delicious meal with brief comments regarding the island, the house, and Prancer. Carrying one tray full of dishes to the kitchen, he returned with a frosty pitcher of iced tea and invited me to the open deck which stretched out over a rock formation.

"It's beautiful here," I said as he gestured to a comfortable chair.

He sat next to me, leaving the cold drink on a white wicker table between us. "I've always loved it," he said.

"This was your home as a child?"

Finn looked to the sea then to me. "Yes, many years ago."

I was quiet for a moment before I spoke. "Molly told me that you'd lived on the island as a child."

Finn smiled. "Molly. How is she? I've missed her."

"She's very well, anxious to see you."

His smile faded and he looked again to the water and the setting sun. "I miss her," he said.

I was quiet for a few minutes then felt it was time to tell him the truth. "You don't have to miss her any longer."

close to you

Finn looked at me, waiting for the explanation.

I placed my glass down on the table and covered my eyes for just a moment before looking at him directly. "Finn, I know about Eve, about Jillian, it's over."

He was quiet for several minutes and I kept still as well.

"What can you tell me? Is Jillian okay?"

"Yes, she's doing fine. She and Eve have left Boston; they've gone out to Phoenix to Eve's mother."

Finn nodded. "I'm glad. That little girl had a pretty serious condition. I'm glad to know she's healed and doing well."

I left a silent space before I continued. "You probably had no way of knowing about the accident."

He looked at me with questions in his expression.

"Eve and Tony were in an automobile accident. Tony didn't make it."

"And Eve wasn't hurt?"

"She was, but not badly. I went to see her at the hospital."

Finn looked confused. "How did you happen to visit her?"

I explained my editor asking me to dig up more on the plane crash that had taken a beloved surgeon away. I'd been to his house for more information, I'd spoken with Eve, and I'd met Molly and Prancer. I related the crime wave of drugs through a perpetrator in Boston. I told him everything non-stop for more than twenty minutes.

When I had covered all the bases, we were both still, the sun setting and the darkness enveloping the skies.

Finn shook his head. "So, the kingpin of this whole thing has been arrested?"

"Yes, he's nothing any longer – there's a list a mile long of his offences. In fact, this article will be in tomorrow's paper. I thought you might like to have a copy," I said, taking it from my pocket and handing it to him.

We had another several minutes of quiet except for the crashing of the waves.

"Are you getting cold?" he asked as he stood. "Maybe the living room would be more comfortable."

I stood, picked up my glass, and walked with him inside, Prancer at our heels.

We both sat in our former seats, Finn looking fatigued. "I can go home," he said.

I smiled. "Yes, that's right. The threat to you is over."

Finn glanced at me, looked around the room, then back at me. "The frightening part was the threat to Jillian and to Molly."

I looked at him with uncertainty.

"The kingpin of it all related to me through Tony that if I didn't cooperate in the transport of drugs, Jillian and Molly would suffer the consequences. I had no choice but to disappear. I waited the first two months out in New York City, then when nothing dark occurred and everything was quiet, I came here."

I sat very still for several minutes; Finn seemed deep in thought.

"Your plane…" I began.

"I had no other option but to let it go into the water."

I closed my eyes for a moment then looked at his troubled expression. "Were you injured?"

Finn looked at me with a slight smile. "Not much. I'd thought it out days ahead. I hated to part with that old aircraft, but in comparison to lives, I had no choice. How did you manage to find me?"

I shifted in my seat. "It was coincidental. I spent time out here on the island as a child and decided to come here when my editor asked me to give your story a rebirth. I chose the motel on the hill, and there you were. When Prancer saw you, he knew what I had been questioning, was it really you. Molly and I discussed often what had influenced your life, where you might be. Neither of us wanted to think you were gone. Once I felt certain that you were here on The Narrows, I had learned much of the reasoning for your concealment. I couldn't be completely honest with anyone, and I certainly couldn't drag you into the web of crime I'd been told of."

"So, no story was written about me – I was actually

wondering what you knew and if I was going to pick up the paper one day and see my name again."

"No. I covered my tracks fairly well. Molly knows you're alive – no one else does. Now it doesn't matter who knows. People have asked about you. Your patients were horrified to think you were lost. Your friends, like Dr. Sanchez, have been heartbroken. Molly was devastated."

Finn looked at me then moved to where I sat. "And you?"

"Me? Well, I found consolation elsewhere."

"You did?" he asked, taken aback.

I laughed. "Yes, Rosie and Ruthie – my two rats."

The relief on his face told me everything my heart yearned to know.

I looked out to the dark sky and then at his beautiful face. "The more I learned about you, the more I wanted to find you."

He waited a moment with a slight smile on his face. "Rats, eh? I like rats. Do you always get this involved in your writing?"

I shook my head no and leaned into him as his arm wrapped around me. "I think we've got something here," he said.

Prancer went over and hopped into the chair where Finn had been sitting. We smiled at the dog's audacity. "He's the real owner of this place," Finn said.

We sat quietly for some time until I asked Finn if he

wouldn't like to call Molly. "She's been so worried and lonely. She's told me so many cute stories about you as you went from a child to a man. She misses you."

He stood, picked up his cell phone, and dialed her number. I could hear every word they said, and I was in tears.

"How are my radishes growing?" he asked before saying hello.

I could hear Molly gasp. "Your radishes are four feet tall and I'm fearful they'll cover my roof soon. You must come and harvest those little suckers."

Finn laughed. "Thanks to our Cara, I have my life back. I'll be in Wellesley on Monday. But sometime soon you have to promise to come and spend a couple of days with us on the Vineyard. You'll enjoy it."

I listened as Molly sobbed then heard her assure Finn that she would love to see his old family home.

When the call ended, Finn asked if I'd like to take a walk or have a glass of wine.

"The walk, then the wine," I said.

We put Prancer's leash on him and went out toward the street where we wouldn't have to worry about rocks and slippery seaweed. The night couldn't have been more perfect – the air was mild, the stars and moon became our lights, and being near to Finn, holding hands, was exquisite.

"There's something you should know," I said. "It's about Eve and your grandmother's emerald necklace.

Eve had it on when she was in the accident; apparently it fell off at the hospital. Molly told me it must have been stolen because you wouldn't have given it away. The police have it now."

Finn was quiet for a moment. "Eve had her weaknesses. My main concern was for Jillian. Having met Tony, I worried; he didn't seem kind. The necklace was my grandmother's, but it was one of many; it actually had a faulty clasp, so that's probably why she lost it. If I report that she took it, she could end up in jail. That might put Jillian in a tough place. She may have taken more – Eve was a conflicted soul – sometimes logical and polite, other times moody and harsh. I think hanging out with Tony and who knows what other felons, she was pretty confused. Whatever she took, we can live without." He looked down at me as we walked and slipped his arm around my waist. "I have you," he said softly. "I don't think Prancer and I need anything else."

> *We are all born for love. It is the principle of existence, and its only end.*
> Benjamin Disraeli - 1804-1881

Made in the USA
Middletown, DE
27 June 2019